Rath

Rath

Herbert J. Shiroff

Publisher's Note
This book is a work of fiction. Names, characters, places, and incidents either are the product of the author's imagination or are used fictitiously, and any resemblance to actual persons, living or dead, business establishments, events or locales is entirely coincidental.

ISBN: 1507842341
ISBN 13: 9781507842348
Library of Congress Control Number: 2015901907
CreateSpace Independent Publishing Platform
North Charleston, South Carolina

In honor of all my grandchildren and all the Raths worldwide.

"You, yourself, as much as anybody in the entire universe, deserve your love and affection."

—Buddha

Acknowledgments

A NUMBER OF PEOPLE GAVE generously of their time, encouragement, and knowledge to assist me in the preparation of this book.

These persons bear no responsibility for any exaggerations, magnifications, conclusions, confusions, or outright errors that appear in this manuscript. All of the foregoing are mine and mine alone. But each person, in his or her own unique way, shares a part in my story.

I would first and foremost like to thank my beloved wife and muse, Andi Shiroff, for all her help, encouragement, and love. I couldn't have written this novel without your participation.

Thanks also to our four wonderful children and their spouses. And most of all, I thank God for our five very blessed and special grandchildren.

To the many Cambodian refugees and their descendants who lived during the times described in this book, I gratefully acknowledge your contributions. Special thanks go to Bruce and Sophia Srey Sharp.

To my many friends and relatives in Pennsylvania, Colorado, and Florida—thank you all for your support.

And finally, I would like to thank Marjorie Lyons, a very special teacher and writer who guided me every step of the way.

Prologue

————

I AM LOOKING INTO THE bright, dark-brown eyes of my eight-month-old Cambodian granddaughter, Rath Mona. No bigger than a newborn puppy, she easily fits inside a metal pretzel can. She looks like a plucked chicken with hair as fine as bird feathers. When she smiles, I melt. She is love to the power of infinity.

This is a story about how I came to know my granddaughter and about the people of Cambodia. It is based on certain events as I recall them.

Certain persons, living and dead, described in this novel are composites of real people. Their names have been changed to protect their privacy.

Introduction

CAMBODIA AND WAR

CAMBODIA'S RECENT HISTORY IS A complicated one, marred by many years of violence and terror. In the 1960s, during the Vietnam War, Cambodia served as a transport route between North and South Vietnam. Because of Cambodia's proximity to Vietnam, the Vietcong army set up bases there. Although Cambodia remained neutral during the war, the presence of these Vietcong bases led the United States to bomb Cambodia. The bombings began in 1969.

In 1975, following the Fall of Saigon and the subsequent reunification of North and South Vietnam, communist forces known as the Khmer Rouge took control of Cambodia. Led by Pol Pot, the Khmer Rouge initiated the most radical restructuring of a society ever attempted. Their objective was to create an agrarian utopia where only farmworkers were valued. Within days, entire cities were evacuated and destroyed. Money and property were deemed worthless. Anyone with an education was imprisoned and ultimately killed. From 1975 through 1979, the Khmer Rouge murdered more than 1.5 million Cambodians.

When the Vietnamese army invaded Cambodia in 1979, many Cambodians fled the country, escaping to refugee camps in Thailand.

More than 100,000 of these refugees later relocated in the United States. Today, there are more than 175,000 people of Cambodian descent living in the United States.

April 1980

———

A LARGE ROUND CLOCK WITH a sweep second hand appeared on the television screen.

Tick, tick, tick, tick, tick, tick...

"Hi. I'm Harry Reasoner."

"Hi. I'm Morley Safer."

"Hi. I'm Mike Wallace."

"Hi. I'm Ed Bradley...and this is *60 Minutes.*"

The next 3,600 ticks would change my life profoundly.

Jennifer

———•———

I MET JENNIFER ON A blind date in 1966. She was adopted at birth through an agency in Delaware. Her biological parents are unknown to her to this day. Jennifer chooses not to seek their identity.

Her adoptive parents, now deceased, were very nurturing and caring people. They also adopted Hope, a second daughter, using the same Delaware agency.

On our first date, we went out to dinner and the movies. We saw *South Pacific*. We enjoyed the film, and after a good-night kiss at her door, I suggested that I would call her again. She encouraged me to do so.

Jennifer was tall, slender, blond, and blue-eyed. She was an accomplished opera singer, but when we first met, singing was not her primary pursuit. A talented painter, she was attending the Hussian School of Art in Philadelphia. She immersed herself in her work. Oils, pastels, watercolors, acrylics—she loved them all. She adored the old masters like Renoir and tried to learn their techniques.

She was a Gemini, born in May. She embraced it all.

At seventeen, Jennifer was not at all experienced in relationships. She had never traveled or lived away from her home and parents.

As time passed, we saw more and more of each other and became more serious. We would go to the park together, hike in the woods, and enjoy being young and in love.

Whenever Jennifer and I would visit family or friends, Jennifer would glow. Her personality, although quiet and somewhat shy, blossomed when she talked about her artwork and her singing. When asked to sing, she would oblige and perform. She had a beautiful voice. I was very proud of her.

I proposed marriage on her eighteenth birthday, and she said yes. Our engagement was to be for one year. We were to have a June wedding!

Jennifer wanted a big wedding. Her parents agreed, and the planning began. For logistical reasons—availability of the clergy, the caterer, the band, and so forth—the date was moved up to December 24, 1967. Christmas Eve.

I didn't mind. I wanted to get married. I was as anxious to tie the knot as she was.

It snowed the night of the wedding. It was a beautiful, romantic affair.

We honeymooned in Miami. The weather was magnificent, the accommodations outstanding, and the food and drink wonderful.

We had a great beginning.

The flight back to Philadelphia was bumpy, and there was ice on the runway when we landed, but we didn't care. We were anxious to begin our lives as Mr. and Mrs.

I went to work; Jennifer went to school and painted in the evenings. We had promised her parents that she would complete her education, a concern they expressed because she was so young. She graduated with honors.

On the weekends we were committed to spend time with our parents—seeing Jennifer's every Sunday and mine whenever we could fit them in. My obligations as a member of the US Army Reserves took up most of my leisure time.

Jennifer wanted to be a professional artist, and I encouraged her to pursue her dream. She set up a studio in our apartment, and she would paint there at all hours of the day and night. She was truly driven to create fine art.

And she was very productive. Her portfolio grew, both in quantity and quality. She began to enter juried art shows. To her joy and satisfaction, she was accepted by her peers. Her work was good and was awarded best-of-show ribbons.

After Jennifer had been showing for about a year, galleries started to inquire about selling her work. They would provide her a place in their gallery where her paintings would be featured. Each gallery offered different arrangements, but most of them requested exclusivity. Jennifer declined their offers. Instead, she decided to pursue less prestigious, less demanding galleries, where her art would be displayed with other artists she knew personally and respected professionally. It never occurred to her that these venues were not necessarily the best marketers of her art.

The galleries that Jennifer chose produced one-woman shows of her paintings. They would advertise the shows locally in the Philadelphia arts media and host openings complete with wine and cheese for the people who came to admire Jennifer's work.

The unspoken purpose of all of this, of course, was to sell the art, not just to put it out there for people to admire. But Jennifer's first eight shows sold just a few prints and no paintings.

Jennifer quickly became discouraged. What was wrong? Was it the quality of her work? Was it her pricing? Was it the galleries she chose?

No one likes to be measured by the numbers, especially a creative person like Jennifer. But that's how she took measure of her career. To her, the lack of sales meant that something was wrong with her work.

"People love your work, Jennifer. Look at the great write-ups you've been getting," I would say. "And the people who come to your shows are crazy about your work. I overheard a conversation at your last show—three couples were positively gushing over your talent."

"That's wonderful, Herb. But great write-ups don't pay the bills. People gushing about my talent doesn't pay the bills. Dollars pay the bills. If they liked my work so much, why didn't they buy any of it?"

"Well, actually, I think one of the couples may have bought a print and—"

"A print!"

"Jennifer. Most artists don't sell very well until they're older."

"Or dead."

"Or dead," I reluctantly agreed.

I tried to convince her not to get discouraged, but to her, the lack of sales meant that something was wrong with her work. All the encouragement she got from her peers in the art world, her professors, her friends, and family meant nothing to her if no one was buying her work.

It was like she was an actress who was always being praised for her excellent auditions, always in the running for the big parts, yet always wound up being edged out by someone else.

It was like auditioning for *American Idol* and not getting the golden ticket to Hollywood.

Fortunately, Jennifer's attention would soon turn from painting to parenting. She became pregnant in the spring of 1969, just as the flowers were beginning to bloom. We were going to be parents!

Now, the emphasis was on learning all about natural childbirth, breathing techniques, dealing with contractions, setting a goal to deliver a baby without the use of drugs, breastfeeding, and so on. We took a couple's class, attending each lesson with mounting enthusiasm. Jennifer went from being a discouraged artist to an excited mother-to-be.

HOPE

Jennifer's sister, Hope, was two years younger. She chose to reach out to her birth parents while Jennifer was pregnant.

After researching Delaware's adoption laws, Hope successfully petitioned the adoption agency where she was born to provide her with the names and addresses of her birth parents.

She wrote identical letters to both her mother and her father, Martha and James. She told them she was their daughter, and if they wished to meet her, she would like to arrange a meeting at their convenience. She included her telephone number and address in the letters. She stated that she had no wish to do them emotional harm; she merely wanted to meet her biological parents.

About a year later, she heard back from her mother. Martha told Hope that she was married, though not to Hope's father. She had a daughter, Susan. Martha wanted to meet Hope.

They met at a local diner. Contrary to Hope's expectations, Martha seemed very young. But she did look a lot like Hope!

Martha told Hope that she had not been married when Hope was born. Unable to care for her newborn daughter, she decided to give Hope up for adoption. "I felt really sad, and I think of you every day of my life with regret that I lost you."

They held each other and cried together.

Hope asked her mother if she knew where her father was. Martha said she did not.

Martha told Hope that Susan, Hope's half sister, lived in Delaware and was married with no children.

Hope told Martha about her life, her adoptive parents, and Jennifer.

All in all it was a good first meeting. They agreed to meet again.

———————

A week before their next scheduled meeting, Hope got a call from Martha. Susan had been killed in an automobile accident.

Martha was distraught. She told Hope she never wanted to see her again. Hope was devastated. Not only had she lost a sister she'd never known, she had lost her birth mother as well.

How We First Got Involved with Cambodia

In April 1970, US and South Vietnamese military forces invaded the nation of Cambodia. I was twenty-seven years old and married, with an infant son and another child on the way.

One by one, my life goals were being achieved. Graduated college, 1964. Obtained a well-paying job in corporate finance. Married Jennifer, 1967. Had our first son, 1970. Two cars. A home in the suburbs. Vacations at the beach and in the mountains. You get the picture.

Then, one Sunday evening in April 1980, everything began to change.

The CBS television newsmagazine program *60 Minutes* did a segment on the Vietnam War. It showed the destruction of property, the suffering of the people, and the utter disregard for humanity on all sides. People were being maimed, children were starving, and villages were being burned to the ground. The report moved Jennifer and me to tears.

When I was in college, I'd observed the protests of the Vietnam War from the sidelines. For some reason I can't explain, I never joined in the demonstrations. Sure, I believed in serving my country, but like so many of my friends, I wanted to avoid the draft. So I joined the US Army Reserves, where I served for six long, stressful years, fearing that my reserve unit would be called to active duty.

I was fortunate. I went through basic training and then underwent advanced training to become a medical corpsman. But I was never called to active service. Instead, every weekend I would go to local meetings for training and every summer I would attend two weeks of "war" camp in Virginia or New York. None of these activities were fun, but they were vastly preferable to doing a tour in Vietnam. This continued until May 1970. I was honorably discharged and very relieved that my military service was over.

After seeing the report on *60 Minutes*, I felt an overwhelming need to do something. To somehow become involved, to help fix the damage we were doing in Southeast Asia. I didn't know how or what I could do, but after discussing my feelings with Jennifer, I wrote a letter to CBS. The essence of the letter was a question: "What could a young American family like ours do to help the people of Southeast Asia?"

One evening, about a month after I'd mailed the letter, I received a telephone call from a CBS producer.

"We've gotten a ton of letters about our program on the war. But yours was special. It was heartfelt and sincere. And it's from Philly, my hometown. That's why I'm calling. If you are interested, please contact a representative, Doris Sill, from the Children's Family Service of the Lutheran Church in Philadelphia—LCFS."

Doris was a delight to meet. A single parent with two sons and a daughter, she was a devoted advocate for refugee resettlement in the United States. Her job with LCFS was to find churches in the area to sponsor refugees from Southeast Asia. With help from the US State Department, LCFS would find newly arrived refugees homes, oversee their language instruction (English), and provide them financial assistance until they could find work. The program interested both Jennifer and me, but we did not belong to a church, and we really wanted to do something as a family—something Jennifer, the children, and I could do together and be truly involved in. I asked Doris if anyone had ever sponsored a refugee to live in their home. She was unaware of this having happened in Philly, but thought it was a good idea.

I advised her that Jennifer and I would like to try this. We would provide food, shelter, and guidance for a deserving person from Southeast Asia.

Little did we know what we were getting ourselves into! Doris took our offer of sponsorship to LCFS, which in turn advised the US State Department. She got back to us about a month later. Her news was positive. We were approved for sponsorship, no problem, but there was a twist—if we agreed to it, we were to sponsor not one refugee, but a married couple, Pinh and Samoen Nit. They were from a rural area in Cambodia, where they had been pig farmers. Samoen had been helpful to the US troops during the Vietnam War. He was unwilling to discuss his duty during the war. I assumed he was pressed into service at a very young age and probably assisted covert special ops on the ground to direct US bombers flying over the country. We were told that they spoke no English. None. Pinh could read and write Khmer, the Cambodian language. Samoen was illiterate.

Pinh and Samoen

———

PICTURE TRAVELING INTO THE FUTURE, to a society far more advanced than your own. That is how I imagine the two refugees from Cambodia must have felt when they arrived at JFK International Airport after an eighteen-hour flight—their first flight anywhere, needless to say—from Southeast Asia.

Pinh and Samoen Nit, each eighteen years old and under five feet tall, walked down the long hallway into the terminal. They were to begin a new life in America. Doris Sill from Lutheran Children and Family Service, Jennifer, and I met them at the gate. We had State Department pictures and the two young refugees had IDs. They looked exhausted but were smiling. Their bright white teeth glistened like seashells in contrast to their dark eyes, hair, and complexions.

We introduced ourselves as best we could. They politely bowed with their palms held together chest high—a very formal greeting.

Their possessions from Cambodia included two passports and two toiletry kits. Each kit contained a toothbrush, a tube of toothpaste, and a comb and a brush. They had a few shirts and pairs of jeans, and a State Department brochure filled with pictures and Khmer writing. That was all they had in the world.

We took them to our car and started on our journey to Pennsylvania. The conversation consisted of oohs and aahs as we traveled along the turnpike and roadway toward home.

Occasionally, Samoen would speak to Pinh in their native tongue, and Doris would attempt to clarify and translate what he was saying, using the picture brochure for reference. As for the two young refugees, they looked out the windows. Images were speeding by them like an old-time kinescope—cars, trucks, trees, fire engines, passing vehicles with dogs hanging out the windows, motorcycles, toll booths. What were they thinking?

Nervous laughter from Pinh would follow Doris's explanations. Jennifer and I were awestruck, as we realized that our communication skills were going to be challenged like never before.

We offered Pinh and Samoen water and peanut-butter crackers. They drank and ate gratefully, though I sensed they were hungrier for something more substantial. I believed that these two young people were not just overwhelmed but culturally very different from Americans. They probably have different notions about asking for things from their hosts, even if what they want is as basic as food and drink. Also, having experienced profound deprivation all their lives, they're used to not having much in their bellies. Unless we offered and they accepted, how would we know?

Surrey Road

———

Two AND A HALF HOURS after we'd pulled out of the airport, we arrived home at Three Surrey Road in Melrose Park, Pennsylvania.

Everyone got out of the car, and suddenly, the whole gang came out to meet us: Pepper, our 150-pound Newfoundland; and our three kids: Greg, age eleven; Drew, age nine; and Molly, age five. Hope had come over to watch them while we went to the airport.

I would have expected Pinh and Samoen to have been overwhelmed by all the commotion. But they seemed quite at ease. The pure innocence of our kids' welcome—hugs and more hugs, and frank, happy chatter—made them smile and laugh. Pepper was wagging her tail and barking loudly while running back and forth. Molly was jumping up and down and shouting, "Hi, Pinh! Hi, Samoen!" Greg, dressed in his Little League uniform, had just come back from practice and was ready for a game of catch. He seemed unsure of what to make of the tumult in the driveway. Drew just wanted to touch our visitors any way he could.

Three Surrey Road was an architect-built English Tudor–style home, approximately one hundred years old. It had character, though we'd picked it up as a handyman special. The previous owners, only the second family to occupy it, evidently had come upon hard times and had let the property decline. Fortunately for us, we had the wherewithal, the imagination, and the drive to fix it up and make it our own. Fresh paint outside and in, a new roof, replacement windows, a new heating system, new insulation, and new bathrooms had done wonders for the place. It was a warm, comforting environment. We were a happy and proud family, and we were very excited to welcome Pinh and Samoen to America and into our home.

We walked through the side entrance of the house into the mudroom. Following our example, Pinh and Samoen removed their shoes and followed everyone into the kitchen.

Pinh's eyes opened wide as she observed the cherry wood cabinets, and the stainless steel and copper pots hanging from the ceiling over the wood block table in the center of the expansive room. Jennifer explained as best she could that this room was where we had our meals. I pointed to the circular antique kitchen table and seven chairs.

Jennifer opened the refrigerator and revealed the contents: milk, fresh fruit and vegetables, leftovers in casserole dishes. She opened the freezer to display ice cream, frozen steaks, French fries, and packages of frozen veggies. Pinh and Samoen got the picture.

All this time, Doris and our kids watched in silence. When Samoen finally said, awkwardly but clearly and with a smile, "Thank you," you could feel the electricity in the air. I'm sure I wasn't the only one to get goose bumps. We were actually communicating.

After that, Doris excused herself. She had to leave. She said that she knew Pinh and Samoen would be happy here and that they were in good hands. We all kissed Doris good-bye, even the kids, and Pinh and Samoen bowed to her respectfully.

After Doris left, Jennifer asked Pinh if she would like to see their bedroom. She pointed to a picture of a bed so Pinh would understand. Pinh nodded yes, and we all proceeded up a circular staircase just off the kitchen to show our new guests their bedroom.

There were two single beds, each neatly made with sheets, comforters, and pillows. Pinh and Samoen oohed and aahed at the sight of their own beds. Molly jumped on one of the beds and said, "Pinh's bed!" Samoen repeated, "Pinh's bed." Pinh laughed. From that time forward, sure enough, that became Pinh's bed. It was the one nearest the window.

We then showed them their bathroom: tub, shower, sink, and toilet.

They didn't seem to understand. But it was now lunchtime, so we decided to wait to explain the bathroom.

We all gathered around the oak table in the kitchen for our first meal together.

Doris had advised us that the recommended beginning diet for Pinh and Samoen was chicken and rice. Of course, once they had become acclimated to their new surroundings, they could eat anything they chose. After all, they were not infants. But their diet in Cambodia had not been very substantial, thus we were advised to take it slow. No hoagies or cheeseburgers for at least a month!

Jennifer took out her wok, along with some cooking oil and rice she'd gotten from the local Asian market. She prepared the rice, and then she cut some chicken breasts into slices and fried them in the wok.

Greg and Drew set seven places at the table with dinner plates, napkins and silverware, and water glasses. Jennifer brought in teacups. She placed the rice in one bowl with a serving spoon and the chicken in another with a serving fork, and brought them to the table. She set out a jar of fish sauce and a bottle of soy sauce. I filled a pitcher with cold water from the tap and topped off everyone's glasses.

Everyone was seated around the table. Molly sat next to Pinh, and Drew and Greg sat on either side of Samoen. Jennifer and I took the remaining seats. Jennifer served Pinh and Samoen first.

As soon as Samoen's plate was filled with food, and before the rest of us could take our portions, he began shoveling the chicken and rice into his mouth with his hands. Pinh did the same after she'd been served. Apparently, they had never used a knife or a fork before. Jennifer gave me a quick glance. We'd have to add manners to our list of things to teach our new guests. But we didn't judge them too harshly. They were obviously very hungry!

"Ugh—gross!" Greg said. "They eat like dogs."

For a moment neither Jennifer nor I said anything in response to our son's comment. Thankfully, Pinh and Samoen hadn't looked up from their food to see Greg's expression, which would have required no translation.

"Hush," Jennifer said. "They're new here. And they're our guests."

"And they're obviously very hungry," I told him.

"Obviously!" Greg said and laughed. He picked up his fork.

"Drew," Jennifer said, "use your fork and knife."

Drew looked terribly disappointed, but he did as his mother said. I did likewise, grinning to myself as I cut up the chicken on my plate. It wasn't bad. The fish sauce made it pretty tasty, actually."

Happy Talk

"Happy talk, keep talking happy talk
Talk about things you like to do
You gotta have a dream, if you don't have a dream
How you gonna have a dream come true?"

—Rodgers and Hammerstein, South Pacific

After our first meal together, Greg and Drew cleared the table, placing the dishes in our large stainless steel sink. I rinsed them and placed them in the dishwasher. There were no leftovers.

Molly led Pinh and Samoen into the living room, where Pepper was stretched out in front of the fireplace. She enjoyed that spot in the summer, as the brick flooring stayed cool. August was not a great month for a Newfoundland, and that August was particularly hot.

Our family had been looking forward to meeting Pinh and Samoen for quite some time. While eagerly awaiting their arrival, we had put together a presentation just for them. Some of it was even in Khmer. Gathering in the living room after lunch gave us a perfect opportunity to begin.

Jennifer began, *"Chum riap sueh. Niak sohk sabbaay te Samoen?"* (Hello, Samoen, how are you?)

Samoen, laughing, answered, *"Kh'myohm sohik sabby."* (I am fine.)

I added, *"'Kh'nyom trawk aw maa dael baan skoal loak."* (We are pleased to meet you.)

Pinh laughed too, and smiled. She repeated my greeting in Khmer. We all cheered! "Hooraaaaay!"

I then asked them if they knew any English. *"Niak jeh phiassa awngle te?"*

They answered together: "No."

Jennifer tried to explain that we hoped to help them learn. They were going to attend a school that taught English as a second language. We had no idea how to relate this information in Khmer, so we tried using pantomime.

As planned, we all began to sing the *South Pacific* song "Happy Talk." We even used hand gestures, moving our fingers and our heads in rhythm to the melody in an attempt to make the song meaningful. Molly thought this was particularly funny and was laughing hysterically. We had practiced for weeks, and I thought we nailed it! Pinh and Samoen seemed to love it, too.

After our song was over, Greg and Drew wanted to go outside. "Dad," they said in unison, "how about we take Pinh and Samoen to Meyers to play?" They had seen enough pantomiming and singing in the living room for one day.

So we all took a break and went outside, going through the kitchen and out the mudroom, down a steep hill to the school across the street. The playground was adjacent to the boys' school, Meyers Elementary. With Pepper leading the way, we crossed the street and entered the schoolyard.

There was a multicolored jungle gym, painted in yellow, red, blue, and green, plus a set of six swings, two slides, and a handball wall in the yard. There was also a basketball court with two backboards, and a ball field where kids could play softball or soccer. For an older public schoolyard, Meyers was one of the best maintained I'd seen. Large shade trees dotted the perimeter of the yard and the school building. It was a lovely facility.

We weren't the only ones there that day. The yard was filled with boys and girls of all ages. Everyone in the playground knew Pepper, and she was in her glory when it came to kids. Her tail wagged happily as Greg's, Drew's, and Molly's friends gathered round to pet her. She was by far the largest dog in the neighborhood and the most kid friendly, too.

Greg and Drew immediately ran off to play handball with their friends. They encouraged Samoen to join them, and he readily agreed. Handball is easy to learn. The other kids hung back while Greg and Drew explained the game to Samoen. He got the hang of it in a few minutes, and the other kids joined back in the game.

Molly only wanted Pinh to push her on the swings. Jennifer helped Molly onto a swing and Pinh gleefully pushed her higher and higher.

I observed the whole playground scene and couldn't have been more proud.

———————

Days turned into weeks.

Before we knew it, thanks to the ESL school in West Philadelphia, Pinh and Samoen were able to speak rudimentary English. Also, as fortune would have it, there was a growing community of Cambodian refugees being sponsored in Philly. Many of them came from the same camp in Thailand as Pinh and Samoen.

Every morning, Jennifer would take Pinh and Samoen to ESL and stay with them until class was over. Meanwhile, Greg and Drew were back at Meyers Elementary and Molly was in nursery school.

Jennifer became more and more interested in the ESL program. Since we were the only family sponsors (all the other refugees were being sponsored by churches and civic groups), she began befriending the various church representatives and Lutheran social workers assigned to the refugees. She also got to know many of the other refugees in the program.

Word began to spread at Lutheran Children Family Service that our sponsorship was achieving unexpected results, all positive. Pinh and Samoen were well adjusted, in excellent health, and happy in their adjustment to their new lives in America. They were becoming more comfortable speaking English and were making friends easily.

Doris asked us if we would be interested in telling our story to other groups—churches, synagogues, civic groups, etc. We said we would like that very much. And so we began to speak of our experience at evening gatherings in our home, encouraging others to pass it on and join in this most rewarding endeavor.

In the meantime, Lutheran found employment for both Pinh and Samoen at a local manufacturing company. They were both to be assemblers of small equipment. Not very exciting work, but it paid each of them an hourly wage. They were on their way to becoming American taxpayers!

Who would have believed it, just a short time ago? You gotta have a dream.

———————

Out

Pinh and Samoen continued to work hard on the assembly line. Their attendance was perfect. They never were absent, and they never were late. They approached the work with enthusiasm, made friends easily, and were liked by all their coworkers. They were real team players.

Precisely six months after Pinh and Samoen started working, I received a call from George, their boss. After exchanging pleasantries, he got down to it.

"I'm calling about Pinh and Samoen. Now, please don't take this the wrong way—they're doing fine work for us, and I don't want you to get alarmed, but..."

"Alarmed? Why—is there a problem? Something they did or didn't do?"

"Not at all, Herb. No problem. I think. I don't know how to say this, but I think they may be having health problems. Lately I've been noticing that their energy levels on the production floor have been slipping. It's like they start running out of gas toward the end of the day. Are they showing signs of fatigue at home?"

"Not that I'm aware of. But I certainly will talk to them and see if I can shed some light on this. I'll also ask Jennifer to get them to the doctor for a checkup."

"Good idea."

"I can tell you this; they haven't required any medical care since they arrived."

"Right. Oh, by the way, I almost forgot to tell you—in spite of their possible health problems we're raising their hourly rate and promoting them to line supervisors. I hope they'll be pleased. They really have learned quickly. I intend to tell them this afternoon, during break time."

"Well, George, you are full of surprises today. You can't imagine how grateful we are for your kindness. Thanks an awful lot."

"You are most welcome. Thank you."

As soon as I hung up with George, I called Jennifer. She had just dropped the kids across the street at Meyers and was about to take Molly to nursery school.

"You're not going believe this, Jennifer, but Pinh and Samoen are getting raises and promotions! Isn't that fantastic? George really likes them. Evidently, they are so proficient that he wants them to supervise each of their production lines. He's going to tell them this afternoon at break time. But—"

"But there is a problem."

"George is concerned about their energy level toward the end of the day. He said they've been looking fatigued. I told him we'd have Dr. Blumberg check them out."

"I'll call him this morning. He has all their baseline test results from when they were processed out of Thailand. Hopefully, he'll be able to see them this evening," said Jennifer.

———————

George met with Pinh and Samoen that afternoon.

They sat across from him at his desk, which was cluttered with paperwork and sample parts taken from the production line for quality inspection. They looked frightened. They had never been called into George's office before.

"Pinh and Samoen. First, please relax. This is a good meeting. You do not have to be afraid," George said.

Pinh replied. "We are happy workers. Samoen and me—we make friends here." Samoen nodded his agreement; he was a man of few words. While Pinh excelled in her ESL classes, the work was less easy for Samoen. He understood English fairly well, but his speaking ability was well behind Pinh's.

George continued. "I want to thank you for your hard work. We are grateful. You have been working here for six months now. I want to give you a pay raise. And a promotion. Do you know what this means? Do you understand?"

Pinh uttered a few words in Khmer and Samoen smiled. Pinh replied to George, "I understand. And yes, Samoen now understands, too. Thank you, George."

———•———

Pinh and Samoen came home and told us excitedly about their promotions.

"Congratulations!" Jennifer exclaimed. "That's great news!"

"Yes. We will make more pay now," Pinh said.

"Well," Jennifer said, "I'm so happy for you. But there was something else I wanted to talk about with you. Come, let's sit in the living room."

"Is there problem?" Pinh asked.

"No. There's no problem. I just have a couple of questions for you."

They all went into the living room. Pinh and Samoen sat on the floor next to Pepper. Jennifer sat on the sofa.

"Pinh, how are you feeling? I know you are happy in your heart about your meeting with George, but how do you feel inside the rest of you? Are you tired?"

Pinh replied. "A little tired after working. Yes."

"OK. Well, I made a meeting with Dr. Blumberg. Do you remember meeting him when you first came to live here?"

"Yes."

"Samoen will meet with him too. OK?"

"OK."

———•———

Jennifer, Pinh, and Samoen arrived at Dr. Blumberg's office at six thirty. The office was located in the front of his home. They went through the foyer into a small waiting area with two large, welcoming sofas, some colorful Tiffany-style reading lamps on dark walnut tables, and a freshwater aquarium bubbling away the silence of the empty room.

They all sat down. A few minutes later, Dr. Blumberg appeared.

"Hello, my friends." He greeted them with a smile and held each of their hands warmly. "Please come with me into my examining office, Pinh and Samoen. I am going to give each of you a health checkup. Jennifer, you may come too, if it's OK with Pinh and Samoen." It was.

He led them into a well-lit room about the size of the waiting room. Only this room was all white and very clean. There were three chairs and a desk, and an upholstered leather table. All white.

"Your health is very important to us, so I am going to do some tests to make certain you are in good health. Have you ever had a health exam before?"

Pinh replied that both she and Samoen had received physical exams in Thailand before coming to the United States.

Dr. Blumberg proceeded with his examinations. First Pinh and then Samoen.

He checked their breathing and their hearts, looked down their throats, checked their teeth and their ears, felt their neck glands, pressed their bellies, tapped their knees, and scratched the bottom of their feet. Each step along the way he explained what he was about to do, what instrument he would use, and that it would not hurt. Finally he came to the part most people dread.

"Pinh and Samoen, we are almost done. But I need to take some blood from your arm."

The doctor drew four vials of blood from each. Neither Pinh nor Samoen flinched. In fact, they watched with great interest as the vials filled.

"I will call you with the results of my exam in a few days."

Pinh and Samoen both said good night to the good doctor and thanked him for seeing them.

———————

"Good morning, Jennifer. Dr. Blumberg here."

"Oh, hi, Dr. Blumberg. How are you?"

"Very well, thanks. I'm calling to let you know the test results are back from the lab. Since you and Herb are Pinh and Samoen's sponsors, I can share them with you."

Jennifer answered in the affirmative. "I already wondered about that, so I checked with the Lutheran Family Service. They told me sponsors can act on their refugees' behalf on all medical related matters."

"Oh, good. Well, would you like to hear the results, or should we wait so I can talk to Pinh and Samoen?"

"No, I'd rather not wait. Please tell me, is everything all right?"

"Not exactly," said Dr. Blumberg. "There is something. But don't be alarmed. Time and the right care will solve both their problems."

"What are you saying, doctor?" Jennifer sensed Dr. Blumberg was not being straight with her. She listened intently with great concern.

"First the bad, which is not really so bad, though it is bad enough. Samoen's blood results were not normal. So I referred them to my associate, Dr. Tang, at Einstein Hospital's Department of Infectious Diseases. Turns out that Dr. Tang sees numbers like Samoen's all too often from Asian refugees. He told me Samoen has parasitic worms, which are causing him to be weak and tired. But—and here's the good news—a couple of doses of the proper medicine and he'll be good as new. Let me give you Dr. Tang's number at Einstein. He said Samoen should be treated as soon as possible."

"What about Pinh?" Jennifer asked, almost expecting more bad news.

"Well," Dr. Blumberg said with a chuckle. "That is not bad news. Your beloved Pinh is...pregnant! That's why she's been getting so tired. Frankly, I don't blame her. I'd be tired, too, if I were working as hard she is while carrying a baby."

"Oh, goodness. I can't believe this. So everything else with Pinh is OK?"

"Everything else with Pinh is unremarkable, meaning she's in very good health. If you like, I can refer her to Dr. German at Einstein. He is an excellent ob-gyn and can guide Pinh on her journey to motherhood no matter what might happen along the way."

"I know him well," Jennifer said. "He delivered Molly."

Jennifer was at once overwhelmed with joy and relieved that her charges were both going to be just fine.

She immediately began thinking about where to put the nursery.

———◆———

Jennifer called me at work with the news from Dr. Blumberg. I nearly fell off my chair. I asked her when she was going to tell Pinh and Samoen. She said she wanted to wait until we were all together as a family. Dinnertime. I agreed.

Before I came home, I stopped at the local florist and got flowers for Pinh and Jennifer. After all, Pinh was going to be a mother, and we were going to be "grand-sponsors"!

———◆———

Dinnertime seemed to come around quickly that day, and the news of Pinh's pregnancy was accepted with a lot of Khmer conversation, a few tears of happiness, and hugs between Jennifer and Pinh. The kids cheered. The ladies loved my flowers. (I even gave one to Molly.)

Of course, we didn't tell Samoen about his condition until the next day. We decided that kind of news was better not shared at the dinner table. He took it well and agreed to go to the hospital for treatment.

———◆———

Jennifer had taken Pinh to the Einstein obstetrician, Dr. German, and enrolled her in a program called "A Better Start." Pinh learned just about everything an expectant mother might need to know. She felt very empowered as a result.

Two doses of the antiparasite medicine were enough to cure Samoen of the worms. Fortunately, his condition was caught before any complications arose. He began regaining his energy immediately.

Everything was going swimmingly. That is, until one evening when Pinh asked us to come together in the living room after dinner.

Pinh had become quite a cook since her arrival in the United States. Her "Better Start" course had added to her skills, and that evening she used her magic wok to make some delicious vegetable tempura. Mushrooms, beans, onions, squash, potatoes—everything was great. Well, of course they tasted better—everything tastes better fried.

The boys were talking about sports and school, and Molly was being a "mosquito," teasing her brothers. Everyone was laughing and enjoying the meal. I was exhausted from a stressful day at the office, and Jennifer just enjoyed having Pinh cook.

After dinner, as Pinh requested, we retired to the living room. "Herb and Jennifer," Pinh began, "Samoen and I have been very happy here in Surrey Road house. We love you all and cherish our time together. But we need to ask if we can get our own house. We have saved money from work and want to buy a house. Will you permit us to do so?"

Jennifer was the first to respond. She was crushed. "Pinh, you have surprised me. Are you sure you want to do this now? What with the baby coming and all? Do you really want to leave us?" Jennifer began to cry.

"I am sure."

"Do you know how much a house costs?" I asked.

"Yes. We found a house in Olney, near Einstein Hospital. It is eight thousand dollars, and we can have some of our friends who we met in ESL school live there with us and pay rent to us. We asked George what he thought, and he told us to ask you."

And so Pinh and Samoen bought a house and began their lives anew, though this time not at Surrey Road. And not with our family.

Tola

———

JENNIFER LEFT TO VOLUNTEER EACH morning before sunrise. Her love for the refugee resettlement program at Lutheran Children and Family Service had become an addiction. She lived and breathed her passion. Twenty-four hours a day, seven days a week, she thought of little else. Her family responsibilities were already secondary to her concern for her clients, the Cambodian refugees. She envisioned herself as a facilitator, a guide helping people to realize the American dream. She gave it everything she had.

She was in a unique situation, as she was the only one volunteering at Lutheran who had sponsored and lived with the people she was now counseling.

She also took a particular interest in one social worker. His name was Tola.

Tola was a thirty-four-year-old Cambodian man. He and his sister, El, had come to the United States as refugees after escaping a death camp in Cambodia. They'd fled into the Cambodian jungle, where they had walked for weeks without food or fresh water. When they finally reached the refugee camp along the border in Thailand, they were near death—dehydrated, malnourished, and exhausted—yet somehow they survived.

Tola came from a wealthy and elite Cambodian family. He'd been educated in France, spoke fluent French and English, and had a very outgoing personality. The escape and subsequent stay in the refugee camp seemed to have had no effect on Tola. While slight of build, he had a fine, well-groomed appearance, and a confident, charismatic air about him.

Jennifer found him charming.

"Jennifer. What a lovely name for such a beautiful woman," Tola said to her when they first met. "I am so very pleased to make your acquaintance. I know we will do wonderful things together."

"That is very nice, Tola. I hope Doris has told you about me and what I hope to achieve here."

"Oh, yes. She has. I know that you and your family have sponsored Pinh and Samoen. Your promotion of sponsorship through your meetings and presentations to various organizations is also of great help. I truly admire your work."

"Thank you. I feel very motivated. There is still so much to do!"

"Well, I am here for you. We can be a very effective team. I hope you'll include me in your life's passion."

———◆———

Our family's successful sponsorship of Pinh and Samoen had caught the media's attention. At the suggestion of the Lutheran Children Family Service and Doris Sill, director of refugee resettlement, we agreed to be interviewed by the local editor of the *Philadelphia Evening Bulletin*. As a result of the publicity, Jennifer and I received numerous invitations to recount our experiences at various churches in the greater Philadelphia area.

In front of hundreds of people, we would review the war in Southeast Asia and how it was affecting Cambodia. We would explain the need for help with the refugees already in Philadelphia and for help with the many more yet to arrive. Our story of Pinh and Samoen was compelling, and we were good at telling it. After all, we had lived it. Jennifer was especially passionate and convincing.

Doris Sill recognized Jennifer's skills. One evening, after our presentation was over, Doris pulled Jennifer and me aside and said, "Jennifer, we at LCFS would like to offer you a paid position working with me and certain social workers at our organization. I'm sure you need to discuss this with Herb, but I really think you'd find the work rewarding."

The ride home that evening was filled with questions.

"Herb, what do you think?"

"Jennifer, I think you were meant for this."

"But what about the children?"

"We'll see if your schedule can be flexible. I'm sure Doris knows we need to consider the kids in all of this."

"Do you think I'm qualified? Am I strong enough to deal with all the problems that might arise?"

"I believe you are. Do you? The decision is yours alone to make. Why don't you sleep on it?"

Jennifer accepted Doris's offer without hesitation the next morning.

———•———

Getting over the emotional disappointment of Pinh and Samoen's decision to leave Surrey Road was surprisingly simple. If Pinh and Samoen no longer required our support and nurturing, we would find others who did. After all, we were now a family committed to helping Cambodian refugees.

Pinh and Samoen's sense of independence and confidence in themselves was a good thing. Their leaving our nest was a positive development. Our relationship would continue. Only in a much more remote way.

Dany Song

———

Siv Heang, also known as Dany Song, was twenty-two years old when she and her one-year-old daughter, Phyda, came to the United States. This was about the same time Pinh and Samoen had arrived. Dany's husband had been a soldier. He gave his life fighting alongside members of the US Special Forces in Vietnam. Phyda never knew her father.

Dany fled Cambodia alone and pregnant. She gave birth to Phyda in the Thailand refugee camp called Khao-i-Dang. Conditions were so horrible in the camp that Dany nearly starved to death. In order to deal with the pain and hunger, she would take cigarette butts and burn the area around her stomach. Scars arranged in a neat circle around her belly remain to remind her of her suffering in the camp. Somehow, the act of burning of her flesh enabled her to survive.

While living in the refugee camp, Dany befriended an American she remembers only as "Joe." He told her he worked for the Central Intelligence Agency, and that he would help her to get to America. Never one to question others, Dany accepted his promise and waited patiently in the camp.

"Joe was a very kind man to me and Phyda. He is the one who gave me my American name Dany Song. He told me that I would have a happy life with a new name."

———•———

Dany and Phyda were not as fortunate as Pinh and Samoen. No one sponsored them. They came to America and were settled in the Logan Refugee House along with eighteen other Cambodian refugees. No personal family was there to greet them at the airport in Newark. Their arrival was nothing like the welcome Pinh and Samoen had gotten from our family.

Dany and Phyda lived in an efficiency apartment on the top floor of a three-story brick building in Logan. They shared a bathroom with all the others. Their home was in effect a one-bathroom boarding house. Still, it was a great deal better than where they had come from.

Jennifer met Dany and the other refugees in Logan as part of her first assignment on her new job. She immediately focused on Dany and Phyda. She thought the young mother and her daughter were beautiful, and she was impressed by Dany's fluency in both English and French as well as Khmer. She knew she wanted to sponsor them and have them live with us at Surrey Road. Maybe Dany could even help her by watching our children while she, Jennifer, was away from home on LCFS business.

———•———

With Doris Sill's permission, Jennifer invited Dany and Phyda to dinner to meet the children and me.

The experience was very different from when we'd first met Pinh and Samoen. There was something sad about Dany's demeanor. Something sympathetic. She seemed to be crying out for help. I imagined her crying out, "Please get me and my daughter out of Logan. Please."

And so we did. About a week after our first meeting, we moved Dany Song and Phyda out of the Logan Refugee House and into Surrey Road. We became sponsors once again.

The Proposal

Dany Song and Phyda flourished living with us at Surrey Road.

Before we knew it, Phyda was an adorable three-year-old, and Dany had blossomed before our eyes into a charming and happy woman. The two partook in all our family activities, yet still found time to celebrate their unique cultural heritage with their Cambodian friends, attending weddings, birthday parties, and various Buddhist holiday festivities.

Then, one Tuesday afternoon, I received a letter at my office from a Mr. Kah Ra. I immediately called Jennifer and read her the letter.

"'Honorable Mr. Herb. Allow me to be Uncle Kah Ra of one Ponh Ra. Write on his behalf am asking permission of you and Miss Jennifer. Ponh Ra is good man. He member Tun Dei Monastery Cambodia and is no longer. Ponh Ra will be high addition to respectful family. I select Siv Heang for Ponh Ra.'"

"I sort of knew this might be coming," Jennifer said after I'd finished reading.

"Knew what was coming? What does this letter mean?" I said. "Who is Kah Ra? Who is Ponh Ra, and why is he writing to us?"

"I have some of the answers, Herb. But I have to run now—we're in the middle of something here. Why don't we meet at Surrey Road around five o'clock, and I'll tell you what I know. Of course, we'll need to talk to Dany afterward."

"Why do we have to talk to Dany?" I asked, but she'd already hung up.

———————

I arrived home before Jennifer.

Dany was in the kitchen with Phyda. She was weeping.

"Dany. Why are you crying? What's wrong?" I asked.

She showed me a piece of paper. On it were several lines of Khmer writing.

"This is why I'm crying. This is what's wrong.

"What does it say?"

"It is from a man I met only one time. His name is Ponh. He demands that I get married to him or he will kill himself."

"What? He has no right to demand anything of you! You are in America. How dare he!" I was having difficulty controlling my anger. The letter I had received earlier was beginning to make sense.

"Dany, try to understand. You don't have to do anything you don't want to do. Jennifer and I are your sponsors here in America. If this man Ponh would like to marry you, he can't just say he's going to marry you and then do it. It must be with your consent. No one else's. Just yours. It is different here in America."

Just then Jennifer arrived and saw me flushed red with anger and Dany still teary-eyed.

"I'm guessing that you didn't wait for me to deal with this, Herb," she said, seemingly annoyed.

"No, Jennifer. Dany got a note from Ponh. I didn't say anything about the letter. I came in from work and found her crying. She's very upset. This man is threatening to kill himself if she doesn't marry him."

"Oh." Jennifer turned to Dany.

"Dany," she said gently, "would you mind if we discussed this together? Herb got a letter today, too. You need to hear it."

"What kind of letter, Herb? Please read it to me," Dany asked.

I read it and Dany cried some more.

Jennifer tried to comfort Dany.

"First of all, Uncle Kah Ra, the writer of the letter Herb received, is a respected elder of the Cambodian community in Philadelphia. I've met him several times at the Lutheran offices. He is a traditionalist who is trying to keep the Cambodian culture alive here in America. You can imagine what a difficult task that must be, given the lack of formal education of many of the refugees we are working with." Jennifer cleared her throat, and then she continued. "It appears that Uncle Kah thinks he is rightfully applying the Asian custom of an arranged marriage. Since he is Ponh's eldest relative, and Herb and I are Dany's sponsors, he assumes we three have the authority and responsibility to arrange a marriage on their behalf. As far as I'm concerned, he can think this all he wants, but the decision must ultimately be left to Dany and Ponh."

"I do not love Ponh," Dany said. "I do not know Ponh. He is very ugly. He has but one eye. He lost his eye and his face was scarred by acid caused in a fight. He has few friends. He was a monk in Cambodia. I do not know why he is no longer a monk. He has no job. He speaks little English. I believe Phyda would fear him. Please, Jennifer. Please, Herb. I don't want to marry Ponh."

"Dany," Jennifer said, "we will do everything we can to help you."

THE MEETING

Early the next day, Jennifer was able to locate Uncle Kah Ra at his apartment in South Philadelphia. Since he had no telephone, she took a chance and paid him a visit in person. He lived in a brick row house. It was modest in size. In the front, three steps up from the sidewalk, was a brown wooden porch in need of fresh paint.

Jennifer climbed the steps and knocked on the ornate glass-and-wood front door. He was at home.

"Good morning, Uncle Kah." Jennifer bowed with her hands together, center front. "May I come in?" He and Jennifer had met at the offices of Lutheran, so he nodded and opened the door for her.

Jennifer entered a small foyer and followed him into the living room. The room was lit with the glare of the sun coming through the front windows. Nonetheless, it seemed dark. The windows needed cleaning. The walls were painted white. No pictures or other artwork were to be found anywhere. A sofa took up most of the space, and a tired-looking rug covered the hardwood floor. A large floor lamp sat in the corner unlit.

Uncle Kah was a slightly built man. His hard life in Cambodia had taken its toll, and he appeared much older than his age of forty-five. His head was shaved, and he appeared monastic in his orange sarong, which was wrapped around his thin frame. His feet were bare.

"I am here to visit you today on behalf of my husband and myself, to request your presence at our home to discuss your letter."

"May I bring Ponh and my friend Tola to this, how you say, discussion?" Uncle Kah asked.

"Of course you may. Yes, absolutely." On the one hand, Jennifer had hoped Uncle Kah would suggest bringing Ponh. She felt awkward suggesting this herself, although she had planned to request Ponh's presence if necessary. She knew if this matter was to be resolved, Ponh had to be confronted in person. The sooner the better. Uncle Kah had made it easy for her.

On the other hand, his bringing Tola to the meeting was unexpected.

Jennifer felt unsure about Tola attending.

Certainly not because of Tola's status as a social worker. He was one of a small number of young, educated, nonclergy Cambodian men who had survived the Khmer Rouge regime and made it to America via Thailand. He was believed to be somehow related to the Royal Family of Cambodia in exile, but this was not discussed or known to be factual.

Tola was a handsome man, always well groomed and dressed in a suit and tie. He was a consultant to the UN Agency for Cambodian Affairs and also worked with Jennifer at the Lutheran Agency. He was polished and well spoken.

I remember thinking that if I were to choose a spouse for Dany Song based solely on his appearance, Tola would have been at the top of my list.

But having Tola at this meeting worried Jennifer. She knew he could be charming and very persuasive. And he was an advocate for Ponh. She feared he might influence Dany's decision.

Nevertheless, Jennifer left Uncle Kah's feeling she'd accomplished what she came to do. She was hopeful that night's meeting would resolve the matter of Ponh's proposal.

———◆———

Wednesday was a school night, so the children were in their pajamas and all ready for bed when everyone arrived at eight o'clock sharp.

Introductions, formal bows, and greetings were exchanged. The kids said good night, left us, and we all sat down together. Sort of.

Uncle Kah had come dressed in jeans and a T-shirt. Ponh had on the same, along with a black eye patch that made him look less menacing than I had imagined he would. Tola was in his customary suit and tie. The three sat on one side of the living room. Jennifer, Dany, and I sat on the other side.

Everyone had serious looks on their faces. There was no smiling, no direct eye contact whatsoever. You could hear a pin drop. It was that quiet, that intense. I decided I'd better start things off.

I rose to speak. Since I was still angry at the audacity of Ponh's bizarre proposal, I had little patience for the discussion taking place especially in my own home.

"Uncle Kah, Tola, Ponh, welcome to our home. Jennifer and I invited you here this evening to discuss what to us is a very important and serious matter. First, let me state that Jennifer and I are Dany Song's and Phyda's sponsors here in America. Dany and Phyda are part of our family. Second, Dany is no longer called Siv Heang. She has legally changed her name here in America to Dany Song. Please call her Dany. Lastly, please understand that we honor and respect your culture and your traditions, but we intend to do everything we can to help Dany and Phyda to have a good life in America."

Tola replied first.

"Thank you, Herb, for your kindness in meeting us here. According to our customs and traditions, the bringing together of a man and a woman for marriage is the responsibility of the parents of the man and the woman. In this instance, Uncle Kah is Ponh Ra's parent representative, and Ponh recognizes you and Jennifer as the parents of Dany."

"We understand," Jennifer said. "Uncle Kah is proposing an arranged marriage between Ponh and Dany. He is requesting our agreement. Correct?"

"Yes, this is so," said Uncle Kah.

"Well," Jennifer said, "in America, the creation of a family is viewed quite differently than in Cambodia. Here, we place value on the feelings of both the man and the woman. There must be consent by both persons. If the woman does not love the man, in America, the woman may not be forced to marry him."

On this point made by Jennifer, I decided to add my views on the matter. I was still angry that we even had to go through all this. So I said, "As Dany's sponsor, I do not agree to this marriage. Dany has advised both Jennifer and me that she does not want to marry Ponh. If you want to hear the reasons, I can give them to you. Or Dany can give them directly to Ponh. As I see it, though, there really isn't anything more here to discuss."

"I know Dany does not know me," Ponh said. "I realize my face and my eye is not good. But this should be unimportant, since it is my spirit which is good. I know I have no job. But I am a fisherman and hope to have a boat soon. I have loved Dany from afar for a very long time. I first saw her in the Thailand camp many years ago, before Phyda was born. If she will know me, in time she will understand and want to marry. Dany, I pray, give me a chance."

"Why don't we give this some time?" Tola said. "Let Ponh and Dany find their way without our interference. I believe they can resolve this together. What do you say, Dany?"

Dany spoke for the first time. "Herb and Jennifer…and Ponh. I am today very afraid. But my belief and faith in doing what is good and right will help me decide what to do. I agree to give this, as Tola said, some time."

After that, what could anyone say? Dany bid good-bye to the three men, and we all said good night.

———

"Well, Dany, that was a surprise," I said. "You actually persuaded Ponh and Uncle Kah to agree to let you decide whether you and Ponh will marry. No more arranged marriage. How are you feeling about that?"

"I'm still afraid."

———

THE COURTSHIP OF PONH AND DANY

The next afternoon, Ponh went to see Dany at her place of workplace. He was dressed in a blue blazer and a white button-down shirt and tie. Cleanly pressed khaki trousers and polished loafers finished off the look.

He walked into Dany's mailroom and all the workers stopped what they were doing. Dany walked over to Ponh and said, "Ponh, hello. What are you doing here? Everyone, this is my friend, Ponh."

"I have come here to ask you to dinner," Ponh said.

"Oh, do you mean tonight?" Dany asked.

"Yes." Ponh was very serious. He nodded to the staff as if to greet them.

"Well, I need to contact Jennifer to see if she can be home tonight with Phyda. If she can, then I suppose we can have dinner." Dany smiled. She was amused that Ponh never thought to telephone her, but instead had simply appeared. She was also very impressed with his appearance. She had never seen him dressed up before. He looked handsome. Even his eye patch seemed OK.

"Ponh, you look very nice. Give me a few minutes to take care of Phyda."

Dany called Jennifer and arranged for coverage for Phyda.

———◆———

Ponh and Dany's first date was very eventful. Ponh drove a small Honda motorbike. Dany sat behind him. It was a mild, warm evening and the wind in her long dark hair was refreshing.

They went to an Asian restaurant in Logan, not too far from where Dany had lived. They sat at a table with a white linen tablecloth covered by glass. The place had only ten tables but was very clean. Evidently, the owner/chef was a friend of Ponh's. He appeared from the kitchen, greeted Ponh warmly, and Ponh introduced Dany as his friend. They spoke in Khmer.

The food was prepared to Dany's liking. Poultry and stir-fried vegetables with lots of fish sauce, salty and flavorful. The conversation was limited to questions from Dany and answers from Ponh.

"Ponh, where are you living?"

"Lehighton, Pennsylvania."

"Where is that?"

"About one hour from here."

"Do you have friends there?"

"Yes."

"Is there work for them there?"

"Yes."

"What kind of work?"

"They find some jobs in a local factory. Only sometimes. Lifting, loading trucks, shipping, helping. It's hard to find work."

"How do you live? Do you have a job?"

"No. But I get money from Pennsylvania Welfare each month. Also food stamps. I am able to save money. I purchased my clothing from the Good Will Store." He smiled. It was clear to Dany that he was very proud of his wardrobe.

"What are you saving money for?"

"A fishing boat."

Ponh went on to tell Dany of his dream of becoming a fisher-man. He explained as best he could that a friend of his had found a place where he could live in Louisiana not too far from New Orleans. Ponh's plan was to move to Louisiana, buy a boat, fish for shrimp, and send for Dany and Phyda once he was able to provide for them.

Dany was starting to gain a favorable impression of Ponh and his ambitions. As he spoke, she imagined living in a Louisiana fishing town with a husband and a father for her daughter. Her thoughts were shattered suddenly when Ponh asked:

"Dany. Do you have money? I want to buy a boat."

Dany was dumbfounded by Ponh's question. His unreserved candor made her feel uncomfortable. How could she feel anything positive about this man when he was constantly surprising her? Was his unusual behavior attributable to a simple mind or just innocence in the ways of courtship? She was bothered by Ponh's implication that he—a man she didn't know, who had no job, who was living on welfare and food stamps and buying his clothing at Goodwill—was basically asking her to give him money so that he can buy a boat.

Dany did not know. Her cultural upbringing taught her not to care. She accepted whatever life offered. If her life was good, her next life would be even better. If she suffered illness, her health the next time around would be sounder. This belief system had enabled Dany to survive the refugee camp and each chapter in her life thus far. No matter what she experienced, she had the inner strength to cope.

Her fatalism helped her survive horrors in Cambodia, yet also could prevent her from taking action to avoid negative entanglements in the United States.

———◆———

Ponh drove Dany back to Surrey Road. She thanked him for dinner, and they said good night.

"I will see you in two weeks. I am going to Louisiana to buy a boat and arrange for where we are to live. I am very happy you will marry me." With that, he rode off into the night.

Dany stood on the curb. She shook her head and smiled. "What do I do now?" she thought. I never agreed to any of this."

———◆———

The next morning, Ponh boarded a Greyhound bus to Louisiana. He took with him a plastic bag containing just a few items of clothing and basic toiletries. In approximately twenty hours he would arrive in New Orleans.

———◆———

Much of the state of Louisiana was formed from sediment washed down the Mississippi River, leaving enormous deltas and vast areas of coastal marsh and swamp. These areas contain a rich and diverse base for supporting wildlife. Birds, frogs, and fish are abundant and varied. In more elevated areas, wildfires help shape the natural landscape, producing extensive areas of pine forest and wet savannas where many species of orchids thrive. In many ways, Louisiana's subtropical climate is a lot like Cambodia's, with long, hot summers and short, mild winters. Rain is frequent throughout the year, with summer being the wettest of the seasons.

Louisiana is an agricultural state. Rice, dairy products, poultry and eggs, sugar cane, cattle, soybeans, and cotton are all produced there. But the state's number one crop is seafood. Approximately 90 percent of the world's supply of crawfish comes from Louisiana.

It was here that Ponh had decided to make his home.

The trip south was uneventful. The twenty-hour bus ride took Ponh through Virginia, Tennessee, Mississippi, and Alabama. There wasn't much to see, though. The bus mainly stuck to high-speed roads, which offered little view of anything besides rest stops and trees. Ponh saw lots and lots of trees.

Ponh bought a T-shirt with the name of the state at each rest stop. He feasted on hot dogs and Cokes. He napped occasionally and did not talk to a single person on the bus. During the ride his thoughts turned to shrimp. And the boat he was going to buy.

The bus arrived about the same time on the clock as when Ponh had left Philadelphia. It was the morning of the next day. Ponh's "friend" Shoe was waiting for him at the bus stop in an old black Ford pickup truck. Ponh and Shoe had never met.

Shoe was a refugee from Cambodia and had been in Louisiana since arriving in America. His sponsor was a Lutheran Church group in New

Orleans. They'd provided Shoe with the usual gifts given to refugees. Shelter, food, clothing, language instruction, and the opportunity to start a new life in America. Shoe embraced his good fortune and chose to become a fisherman. He was hardworking, honest, and ambitious. He dreamed of having his own boat and raising a family. He knew he could not achieve this alone. Ponh had similar aspirations. Tola knew both men and arranged for them to meet.

———◆———

The Louisiana shrimp industry, which accounts for over half of the total Louisiana seafood harvest, is fraught with problems that have far-reaching economic and social implications. One of these problems is the overcapitalization of the fishery. Simply put, there are too many fishermen relative to the amount of shrimp available for harvest. This has reduced profits and has made it increasingly difficult for many fishermen to stay in business. In addition, imported shrimp from Latin America and Asia have driven down domestic prices. Ponh and Shoe knew nothing about this. They were like-minded. They wanted to buy a boat, and they wanted to fish for shrimp.

———◆———

When he saw a Cambodian man out in the parking lot who appeared to be looking for someone, Ponh got up and walked slowly down the aisle and exited the bus.

Shoe told Ponh he had a truck. "We will be going to my apartment first to drop off your things."

"I have very little," Ponh said and showed Shoe his plastic bag and the sundry T-shirts he had purchased along the bus route. Shoe laughed and Ponh began to relax.

"I think I like it here already," he thought. He realized Shoe looked a lot like him.

They got into the truck and proceeded to drive to Shoe's place.

Shoe and Ponh

LOCATED ABOVE THE MORGAN CITY General Store, Shoe's apartment was only a few minutes' drive from the bus stop. A red canvas awning shaded the brick building's storefront window from the sun. The store carried all kinds of groceries and sundry household items. It also carried nautical supplies, fishing nets and tackle, and just about any kind of bait a fisherman might require. In fact, several fishermen were there just then. Shoe greeted two of them.

"Pete, Joe, I'd like you to say hello to my friend, Ponh. He and I are going into the shrimp business."

Pete was a heavyset African American man. With a shaved head and a muscular build, he reminded Ponh of a fellow monk from his former temple back in Cambodia, only without the traditional orange robe. Just blue overalls and a white T-shirt for Pete. He did have the look of a holy man, however. He had serious, deep-set dark eyes and a contented smile.

Joe was white and of slender build. He had the look of a man who worked long hours out in the sun. Beard stubble poked from his reddish, wrinkled skin. He wore his hair buzz cut, military style. He just stared at Shoe and Ponh, expressionless.

"Howdy, Ponh," said Pete. "Where you from, boy?"

"Pennsylvania," Ponh said. "I learned to shrimp when I was younger, back home in Cambodia," he added.

"Well, good luck, you two," Pete said heartily. "You'll certainly need to work hard. Not an easy life, you know."

Shoe nodded and smiled, and pointed toward the wooden stairs at the back of the store. "See ya, Pete."

Ponh followed Shoe up to the second floor. At the top of the stairs was a locked green door, newly painted by Shoe in anticipation of Ponh's arrival. Shoe unlocked the door and welcomed Ponh into his home.

The apartment was clean and orderly. It consisted of one room and a bathroom. Two windows looked out on the land behind the store, as well as a nearby boat dock. Brightly colored Cambodian silk shades covered the windows. Figures of sea creatures appeared to be swimming up and down the shades. There was one light fixture in the center of the white ceiling. The walls were painted pale blue and looked to be in good shape. A bed was placed in one corner of the apartment and a sofa sat at the opposite end of the room. A bookshelf held some dishes, some books, and a radio. A kitchen table and a countertop with a sink, small refrigerator, and stove completed the room.

"Ponh. This is my home. I would like you to live here, too," Shoe said. "What do you say?"

Ponh said, "We need to buy a boat. When we do so, then I would like it."

"Did you bring money to buy a boat, Ponh?"

"No, I did not. But my wife, Dany, will come with money soon. We need to buy a boat to show Dany. Then she will give money."

"I understand, Ponh," Shoe said. "I believe the boat we want is located near here in a used boatyard. Would you like to see it today? If you like it as much as I do, we can begin our shrimp business very soon."

Ponh said, "I am ready."

———————

Shoe drove them down the road a piece to the Morgan City Used Boat Store. There were a dozen or so fishing boats for sale, lined up in a row in slips along the dock.

Forrest Blanch, a retired fisherman and longtime Louisiana resident, owned the store. He knew Shoe well. In fact, he was a member of the congregation that had sponsored Shoe to come to America. He was almost eighty years old. The sun and the fisherman's lifestyle had taken its toll on his body. He had a forward-bent posture when he walked, as if he were bracing against the wind even when it was still. His face was scarred and red from the sun and the blowing sand.

"Good morning, Shoe. How are you today?" Forrest asked.

"I am fine, kind sir." Shoe bowed respectfully to the old man. "I want you to meet Ponh. He is to be my partner in the shrimp business."

"Pleased to make your acquaintance, Ponh," Forrest said. He extended his hand, and he and Ponh shook.

"Hello," said Ponh. "We are here to buy a boat."

"I am well aware you are here to buy a boat, Ponh," said Forrest, smiling. His two shiny gold teeth glistened in the sunlight. "The size of a captain's shrimping boat represents an investment and commitment to fishing as a livelihood. The larger the vessel, the more the fisherman has an economic stake in the industry. We have small boats, medium boats, and large boats. About one third of all the shrimp boats here in Louisiana are small, about forty feet. About one third are medium, about fifty feet. And about one third are large, over sixty feet. Do you and Shoe have thoughts on the size of the boat you'd like?"

Ponh shook his head. He had never given the boat size any thought. Ponh and Shoe had never discussed any details regarding their arrangement. All Ponh knew was he wanted to be a shrimper, and for that he needed a boat. Fortunately for Ponh, Shoe was prepared for Forrest's question.

"I believe we are in need of a medium boat. Fifty feet. Since two of us will be working, it seems to be a good size. Do you agree, Forrest?" Shoe asked.

"I do. As a matter of fact, I have the perfect boat for you. It is forty-eight feet, well equipped, and in excellent repair. Financing is available from the local bank, too. I am aware of your circumstances and am prepared to vouch for your creditworthiness. Now, why don't we take a look at her?"

Forrest led Shoe and Ponh along the dock to the slip marked #4. The boat looked beautiful to both prospective buyers. Shoe asked if they could go aboard.

"Of course," said Forrest. "Would you like to take her out?"

"How much does this boat cost?" Shoe asked.

"Why don't we worry about that later?" Forrest replied.

"But, kind sir, we have no money with us. Ponh has a wife with money in Pennsylvania, but we have no money here now," said Shoe.

"I understand, Shoe. Let's worry about the money after you and Ponh decide if you like the boat. OK?"

They got on board. Forrest showed Shoe how to start the engine. Ponh manned the throttle and the wheel. Ponh backed the boat out of the dock. The engine sounded like a tiger roaring and the boat seemed agreeable to Ponh's command.

Shoe manned the engine while Ponh steered the boat per Forrest's directions. They were going to the fishing estuary. These tidal inlets, where the seawater mixes with fresh water derived from land drainage, teem with sea life, including shrimp.

Shoe's and Ponh's test-drive into the estuary went as smooth as glass. Forrest was determined to make their first experience a positive one. During the ride he guided them in the workings of the vessel. He reviewed the workings of the trawling nets used to catch the shrimp. He showed them where the blast freezer with two icemakers was located. He demonstrated how to freeze the catch with chill plates in the boat's fish hold. This would keep the fruits of their labor fresh for delivery to market.

Forrest continued the lesson. He explained about the two primary shrimp species harvested in Louisiana. Both brown shrimp and white shrimp spawn in offshore waters of the Gulf of Mexico. Once hatched, the young migrate inward with the help of the currents to inhabit coastal estuaries. The fact that there are two kinds of shrimp enables the fisherman to work in all seasons—summer, fall, winter, and spring.

Brown shrimp begin their migration to the estuaries during late winter. Once there, they feed and grow until early summer. As they begin their trip back to the Gulf spawning grounds, they are available for harvest while still relatively small and in inshore waters.

White shrimp follow a similar pattern in the Gulf, but don't reach the estuaries until early summer. They feed and grow through midautumn. When the water temperature begins to drop, they begin their migration to the Gulf and become available for harvest. During the spring, as water temperatures begin to rise, some juvenile shrimp reenter the estuaries, where they grow into subadults and are available for harvest during the spring and early summer. Inshore waters are open to white shrimping from late summer through early winter.

After a few hours of cruising the estuary, they turned about and headed back to the dock.

"We are most grateful for your guidance, Forrest," said Shoe.

"I am very pleased," said Ponh.

Forrest directed Shoe, who was now piloting the boat, into the slip. Ponh grabbed the rope lines and secured the vessel to the dock.

Shoe and Ponh disembarked with a spring in their step. They were on the way to living their dream.

Ponh, the Former Monk

SHOE AND PONH HEADED BACK from the boat dock to the Morgan City General Store. Neither of them said a word until Shoe had parked his truck.

"I don't know about you, Ponh, but I am really thirsty," Shoe said. Ponh nodded, and they stopped in the store and bought two Cokes. Shoe paid for them. Then they went back outside and sat on the wooden bench in front of the store and quenched their thirst.

"Well, Ponh, how are you feeling about today's visit to see the boat?" Shoe asked. He took a gulp of his Coca-Cola.

"I like the boat very much," Ponh said.

"Do you believe the boat is the right one for us?"

Ponh hesitated. "Before I answer, would you like to know me? It is important to me that you know me. I believe I am very different from you...Our lives and experiences are not the same..."

"Yes, I know this," said Shoe.

"Please, allow me to explain," said Ponh.

Shoe turned to face Ponh. For the first time since they had met, Ponh was about to talk about himself.

"Please begin, Ponh. I am most interested in what you have to tell."

Ponh took a deep breath and began. "As you know, I was a Buddhist monk in our homeland. Buddha once said, 'You yourself, as much as anybody in the entire universe, deserve your love and affection.' I want to believe this without question. I need you to know me.

"When I lived in Cambodia, before the war, our temple was the heart of village life. And I was at peace. One of my responsibilities was to perform a defining ritual of Buddhism: the early morning walk through the community to collect food.

"One morning, in the matter of a few seconds, my life changed from the sacred to the profane."

Shoe was captivated by Ponh's words. He had never suspected Ponh could be so articulate.

Ponh continued, animated yet calm. As he spoke, he reached out his hands in front of him, gesturing. He was finally telling his story to a friend.

"I was walking back toward the temple with an armload of firewood, when a man stepped in front of me. The man held a glass in his hand. I thought he was offering me a drink of wine. I stopped to greet him and bless him in advance of his offering. But he wasn't offering me wine. Instead, he threw the contents of the glass into my face. What I had thought was wine was in fact acid. And the man was not a believer, but someone else. The acid burned my eye and the skin on my face. I screamed in pain and cried out for help. Then I collapsed in the street.

"I woke up in the village clinic. A doctor had been summoned from Phnom Penh. He told me I had lost my eye from the acid burns, but my life was spared and the scars on my face would heal given enough time.

"Buddha says, 'Peace comes from within. Do not seek it from without.' But how was I to continue my life? I was in pain. Someone I did not know had disfigured me, and for a reason I did not understand. I was very hurt and very angry.

"And so I sought refuge in prayer, study, and meditation.

"My life was a portrait of traditional Buddhist asceticism. I lived in a remote part of Cambodia in a thatched house on a river connected to the shore by a rickety wooden bridge. I had no furniture, and I slept on a wooden floor. Every morning I would awaken while the mist on the river was still evaporating. Then I would attend prayers with my fellow monks. Every morning. We would chant, 'Do not believe in anything simply because you have heard it. Do not believe in anything simply because it is spoken and rumored by many. Do not believe in anything simply because it is found written in your religious books. Do not believe in anything merely on the authority of your teachers and elders. Do not believe in traditions because they have been handed down for many generations. But after observation and analysis, when you find that anything agrees with reason and is conducive to the good and benefit of one and all, accept it and live up to it.' So taught Buddha.

"I learned that everything changes. Our actions are our true belongings, the ground upon which we stand. After much prayer and consultation with my inner self, I decided to leave the temple and return to the secular life.

"Shortly after I left the temple, Pol Pot and the Khmer Rouge came to power."

Shoe responded, "Ponh, my dear friend, my brother. You have moved me to tears. I want to know more. I see this has been difficult for you to tell me. When you are ready to tell me more, we will have many hours together. Your words are just beginning to flow toward me, as water flows in a stream after a rain. Please understand that I would like to respond to your words by sharing words about my life, so you may better know me, too."

Ponh received Shoe's heartfelt comments by coming close to him and touching his hands. "Please tell me, Shoe. I want to hear you speak."

Ponh had been through hell in Cambodia and the idea that a man could openly express his pain was very meaningful to him.

The two men then looked into one another's eyes. Shoe looked at Ponh's face and sensed a man desperately seeking friendship. He looked past Ponh's scars and lone eye and saw a caring human being, a man trying to find his way in a new life.

———

Shoe began his story.

"I am much younger than you, Ponh. By the time I was born, the war was already ending. But I am aware of the hardship and the suffering that you have endured. My life has been difficult, too, but overall, I have been blessed throughout my time here on earth.

"Nevertheless, I was born at a time of great poverty. My parents were said to be rice farmers. I never knew them. Times were so difficult that often families had to sell their youngest children so the remaining members would not starve. I was one of those children.

"My parents received money to buy food for one year in exchange for giving me to the Buddhist temple. They were instructed to place me wrapped in a cloth on the front steps of the temple. I was very young, very feeble, and malnourished. A monk lifted me from the step and then delivered me to an orphanage named Pursat. I was perhaps one or two years old—I don't know for sure. I also don't know how many siblings I might have had. I don't know what became of my parents.

"The custom in the village was for the headmaster of the children's home to receive the child and to post a picture on the village square bulletin board immediately after the child arrived. If no one came forward to claim the child after forty days, the child was deemed an orphan. I am certain my parents loved me. That is why they placed me with Buddha. If they had tried to raise me themselves, I most certainly would have starved and died."

———◆———

"At any given time, there were between twenty and forty children in the home. We grew up poor, but we were always fed, clothed, bathed, and loved by our caregivers. We also received training so that we might someday be self-sufficient.

"As soon as we were old enough, the boys were taught to read and write, and to farm and fish. The girls were taught to read and write, and to cook and sew.

"I remember that the orphanage occupied a one-story cinder-block building about the size of ten small rooms. The floors were wooden and covered with straw. The building was divided up into a nursery for the babies, a playroom, a sleeping section where the older children slept on floor mats, and a combination kitchen and dining room where everyone was fed. Bathing and toilets were outside the building. There always seemed to be enough room, no matter how many children there were. We never really knew what 'enough' meant. We were just grateful to be alive.

"Periodically, people from outside of Cambodia would visit. I learned that the visitors were there to take the children for adoption—away to a new home in a new country with a new family. These visitors would meet with our caregivers and then would meet with some of the younger children.

"As I grew older, I believed that I might never be adopted because I was too old. I had been too sickly as an infant. The visitors always seemed to desire the youngest. Because of this, I was often very sad.

"Then one day, when I was about twelve years old, a man named Bill and a woman named Nancy came to Pursat. The man was very tall and very thin. He wore the most beautiful pair of cowboy boots. He was dressed in blue jeans and a white button-down shirt. The boots made him look even taller. He also wore a baseball cap. Nancy, his wife, was also very tall and thin. She had yellow hair and wore a white shirt and a long white skirt. Her white shoes were Nike and were covered by her long skirt. Evidently, they had come from the United States to meet me."

The News

"We are at once beautiful and proud...and
at once disassembled and broken."

Julio C. Garcia, Painter

It was a sunny morning in May. I was in my office, working on the computer, when Dany Song came by.

Dany was dressed in blue jeans and a green T-shirt, the usual garb for the company's mailroom workers. She was in charge of the mailroom staff, all fourteen of them, and she reported directly to me. She was a very reliable employee, with perfect attendance and an excellent work ethic. She had earned her position of responsibility through hard work.

That she had lived at Surrey Road with my family and that I was her sponsor did not hurt, but it really was not a factor in her career growth. I was as proud of her achievements as a father would be of his own daughter's. And I loved her as a father would. I only hoped the best for all of my children.

I smiled. "What can I do for you today, Dany? How's it going?"

"Everything is not fine. Herb, I have some very serious news for you."

"Whatever could that be, Dany?"

"I am telling you this because I think you should know what is happening."

"What do you mean? What are you talking about?"

For a moment, Dany looked at the floor. Then she looked up at me again.

"You need to know that Jennifer is having a friendship with Tola."

"Do you mean they are friends?"

"Yes."

"Dany. I know that they work together at the Lutheran offices. And I believe there is really nothing wrong with two people being friends. Even a man and a woman. After all, you and I are friends, aren't we?"

"Yes, but we are not having sex."

"What? Are you kidding me? My wife—Jennifer—is having an affair with Tola?"

"Yes."

"Are you sure? How do you know this, for a fact?"

"Because Tola told Ponh, and Ponh told me."

"Ponh," I said.

"You know Ponh is in Louisiana trying to buy a boat. Tola introduced him to this Cambodian man down there named Shoe. Ponh called me this morning and told me about the boat and about Shoe. Then he told me the news from Tola. Ponh also invited Phyda and me to visit next week."

"Oh." I didn't know what to say next.

"What are you going to do, Herb?" Dany asked.

"I don't know."

My face became flushed, and I suddenly felt nauseated.

"I am very surprised. I am hurt, angry, shocked. I never thought Jennifer...Why, Tola played basketball with the kids the other night after dinner. He was a guest in our home. Unbelievable! I am going to call Jennifer and confront her this afternoon. It can't be true. I hope it's not true. It can't be."

I then excused myself and ran to the bathroom to throw up.

———◆———

I reached Jennifer at her office and suggested we meet at Surrey Road.

"Jennifer, something very urgent and important has come to my attention, and I need to talk to you about it away from the office. Can you meet me at home around three o'clock?"

———◆———

Jennifer and I sat across from one another at the kitchen table. She had no idea why I'd asked her to meet me. All she knew was what I'd told her. It was urgent.

I began.

"Jennifer. Someone came to me at the office this morning and told me some very troubling news."

"What was it, Herb? I hope no one we know is ill or anything."

"No. Nothing like that."

"Well, what is it?"

"OK," I said. I took a deep breath. I didn't know if I could say it, but…

"Jennifer, are you having an affair? Are you being unfaithful to our marriage? To our family? To me?"

Jennifer's face immediately turned from pale pink to bright red. "Who told you this?"

"Doesn't matter who told me. Is it true?"

I teared up, ready to cry. She cried first.

"No," she said. Then she got up and left the house.

"Where are you going?" I shouted as she headed for her car. "Is that all you have to say?

No? Please talk to me. Please." I was crying now, real tears.

"I need time alone," she shouted back.

I didn't know what to think. I just sat there, frozen in self-pity and puzzlement.

Jennifer's Poem

JENNIFER AND I HAD BEEN married for over twelve years when Dany told me about Jennifer's infidelity. The fact that she left our home in such distress after I'd confronted her did little to reassure me that maybe, just maybe, Ponh had gotten it wrong.

Jennifer telephoned me about an hour later. I was still at home. "Herb, I know how horrible you must feel. I am very distressed you found out the way you did."

"So you're admitting that it's true."

She didn't answer.

"Are you even sorry about this? Or are you just sorry you got caught? Are you coming home so that we can discuss this? Please, I need to talk to you."

Again, there was silence on the other end of the line.

I could feel my blood pressure rising. My heart was pounding. Was I angry? Oh, yes, I was angry. Deep down inside, I had a feeling that it was hopeless, that my marriage could never be saved. But I was determined to try. After all, we had three kids together, a home we both loved. We had a great family. I loved her.

"Jennifer, how about we find a professional counselor to help us through this."

More silence. Then, at last, Jennifer spoke. "Herb, I need time away from home. From you. From the children. I am going to live in an apartment not too far from Surrey Road. I will agree to see a counselor if you find one. But for now, I need space. I hope someday you will understand. Good-bye, Herb. I will call you later."

I called the office to tell them I would not be returning that afternoon. I needed time to focus on what had just happened.

When the children came home from school, I told them that their mother had to go out of town on a business trip. She wouldn't be home for dinner or to tuck them into bed. She wouldn't even be there for them the next morning. I didn't like lying to my kids, especially having to cover for Jennifer. But I did it nonetheless, to protect them from the hurt and pain that were sure to come when they found out the truth.

"Mommy asked me to tell you that she'll call later," I told them. The kids seemed to take the news in stride, even though it was the first time it was Jennifer who was away, not me.

"So where would you guys like to have dinner?" I asked.

"McDonald's!"

"OK. Everybody do your homework before dinner time, and we'll all go," I exclaimed, doing my best to sound happy about it.

"Can Dany and Phyda go, too?" Molly asked.

"Of course they can," I said.

Dear Herb:

I never loved you fully
Although three children we have raised
I protected my heart truly
Always one foot off the ground
I got lost in our maze

I keep searching for the right
But it keeps avoiding me
I have sorrow in my soul
Wrong really loves my company

I don't want to take away your life
I don't want to be your wife
I know it kills you deep inside
I don't want to be the reason why

This is more than love, it's our destiny.

Jennifer

OUR FIRST NIGHT WITHOUT JENNIFER

After the kids had finished their homework, they piled into our Toyota wagon, and we all rode to McDonald's. I drove with Greg alongside me in the front. Dany and Drew sat in the midcabin seats, and Molly and Phyda sat in the rear. As was the custom when we rode together, Molly and Phyda began to sing.

"Front wheel broken, axle draggin'. You can't ride in my red wagon. Click, clack, click, and clack. Second verse, same as the first, a little bit louder and a whole lot worse." And so on, until we arrived at the restaurant.

"Dad, I'm getting a little old for this," Greg said.

"Deal with it, Greg," I told him. "You're really not that old. Being twelve should be fun. Go with the flow. Be a duck. Enjoy your sister. Remember, you were once Molly's age. She's five now, but just wait until she's a teenager. Then you'll understand."

I knew that, of all the children, Greg was going to be most affected by the separation. After all, he was the firstborn. He was probably more in touch with Jennifer's feelings than the others, though. I wouldn't be surprised if he'd sensed Jennifer's unhappiness for a long time.

Anyway, we all liked eating at McDonald's, and it made me feel good to see everyone having fun. I ordered four Happy Meals with chocolate milk for the kids, and two Big Macs with vanilla shakes for Dany and me.

NANCY AND DR. VESPA

After dinner, I called Nancy, the daughter of a dear family friend. Nancy sort of played a big sister for me. She also worked in my office.

"Hello, Nancy, this is Herb. How are you? Listen, I need to ask you to do me a favor. I know you'll be discreet when I tell you what's happening."

"Of course I will. You know that. What's going on?"

"No one knows this yet, but Jennifer and I are separated. Very sudden. Very unexpected. I suggested to her that we seek counseling, and she agreed. Do you know anyone we might use?"

"I'm so sorry, Herb," Nancy said. "Do the children know? You must be truly bummed out!"

"That is an understatement. And no, the kids know nothing at this point. I'm waiting for the right time to tell them, but there probably isn't one. I just have to tell them."

"Well, I do know someone you can talk to. My ex and I saw this psychologist for nearly six months before we finally split. Dr. Vespa. I guess the failure of our marriage speaks for itself, but that had nothing to do with anything he did. I thought he was very professional. He helped us stay relatively civil to one another. I can give you his contact information if you like. Feel free to reference me. I consider him a friend."

———•———

"Doctor Vespa's office. This is Sally. How may I help you?"

"Hello, Sally, my name is Herb. Dr. Vespa was referred to me by Nancy Blue. I believe she was a patient of his a while back. Is he available? I need to speak with him."

"Do you need to make an appointment?"

"Yes, I would like to make an appointment, but I want to talk to him first. Is that possible?"

"Not really. He'll be in with clients all day long. That's why I'm here. Our policy is that first Dr. Vespa meets with you. If you feel comfortable with him after a one-hour consultation, then you will become his client."

"But this may be for both me and my wife."

"Not unusual. Why don't we set up an appointment for the two of you now?"

"OK. What time can you see us?"

"How about seven o'clock on Thursday evening?"

I gave Sally our names and insurance information, and told her I would contact Jennifer.

"If Jennifer agrees, we'll be there. If not, I'll call you back and let you know."

"That will be fine, Herb. See you on Thursday."

———•———

I called Jennifer's office. She didn't take the call, so I left her a message, including the when and where for our first meeting with Dr. Vespa. I asked that she call me to confirm. We could meet at Vespa's office.

Jennifer called me back and left a message. "Thursday at seven will be fine, Herb. I know exactly where Dr. Vespa's office is located. See you there."

———————

Dr. Vespa greeted us with a pleasant smile. He looked to be around fifty. He was about six feet tall and had a slim build. He wore wire-rimmed half glasses that sat at the tip of his rather large nose. His black hair was intermixed with silver and gray. It was receding in the front but he wore it long, gathered into a shoulder-length ponytail. He had piercing blue eyes and wore a sport coat with no tie. He looked like a marriage counselor, I thought. I liked him right away.

Jennifer was already seated before Dr. Vespa's desk when I arrived.

"Hello, Herb," she said coldly.

"Nice to see you, Jennifer," I replied.

Dr. Vespa welcomed me and pointed me to the chair next to Jennifer. He took his place behind his desk.

"Folks, how can I help you?"

For a moment, neither of us spoke. Dr. Vespa tried a different tack. "Herb, why don't you start?"

"OK. I'm hoping that you can be of assistance to Jennifer and me. We have been married for over twelve years. We are now separated, and I don't know what to do. Our children are living with me in our home, and Jennifer has an apartment. She just up and left." As I finished, tears rolled down my cheeks.

Dr. Vespa looked at Jennifer. Her face was red, stiff, expressionless. She just sat there, looking forward into space, her hands folded in front of her chest. Dr. Vespa asked her if she would like to tell her view of the meeting.

Jennifer replied. "I don't know if I want to…" she began. "It's very complicated. We view things very differently. Herb thinks everything is black or white. I am an artist, and I see things more in shades of gray."

"Very well said. Let's see, now; the question was how could I help you. Herb, you asked for assistance from me. Jennifer, you appeared hesitant to participate. Would you feel more at ease if Herb left the room for a few minutes?"

Jennifer nodded. "Yes, I would."

I was not surprised. Jennifer hated confrontations.

"Herb, would you mind going into the waiting room while Jennifer and I speak to each other? We'll not be too long. I've got some really good sports magazines out there to read while you wait."

———— • ————

After about thirty minutes, Dr. Vespa came out of his office. "Please come back into my office, Herb. Jennifer is no longer here. She left out a private exit."

I followed him back into his office. As I sat down across from him in the same chair I'd sat in earlier, I glanced over at the empty one beside me. I put my hand to the seat. It was still warm. Jennifer must have left just a moment ago. I had a very bad feeling as I waited for Dr. Vespa to speak.

He coughed a nervous cough and sighed. "Herb, I'm really sorry, but in my professional opinion, your marriage is irretrievably broken."

"What do you mean, Dr. Vespa? Can you clarify how you know this in less than an hour after meeting us?"

"Yes, I could. But I won't. Let's just agree to work together to get your life pointed in the right direction. You seem like a good guy, but a hurting guy. By the way, I talked to Nancy for some background on you. Nothing personal, all aboveboard, and all positive. She thinks very highly of you. Anyway, suffice it to say that Jennifer has chosen a life path that will provide her with fulfillment in a new and different way. That life path does not include you."

"What about the children? Does it include them?"

"Jennifer's role with the children will evolve over time. For now, you will be the custodial parent. What do you say, Herb? Shall we work together?"

"That's a lot of information to take in," I said. "I wasn't expecting to have counseling alone, but…I know I need it. And I can only benefit from it. How do you work with someone like me?"

"You've got to trust me, Herb," Dr. Vespa said. "I am a health care professional specializing in family counseling. I make a very good living because what I do is in demand, and I am good at doing it. I can help you."

I glanced at the clock. "I guess our time's almost up," I said and dug in my pocket for my wallet. Dr. Vespa put his hand up for me to stop.

"Our time tonight is indeed up. But I will not charge you for this session. In any case, you don't have to pay me at the end of each session. Sally will send you a bill in the mail."

I stood up. Dr. Vespa followed suit and offered me his hand. We shook.

"My job is to help you to get through this as painlessly as possible. Although there will be pain, for both you and your family. Can you return tomorrow evening so we may begin? Same time, seven o'clock."

I nodded. "Yes, that works. Thank you, Dr. Vespa, and good night. I'll see you tomorrow at seven."

———— ◆ ————

I felt emotionally drained. What could Jennifer have possibly told Dr. Vespa that convinced him so quickly to conclude that our marriage was over? It boggled my mind. But I knew in my gut that he was right, and I knew I had to move forward and not dwell on what was past.

I drove home a tired and deflated man. How would I face the future? Would I have the inner strength to prevail? Would Dr. Vespa be the right counselor for me? For the children? Questions and more questions. Only time would provide the answers.

———— ◆ ————

Friday evening came quickly. Dr. Vespa was waiting for me when I arrived at his office. We exchanged greetings and took our seats, and Dr. Vespa began. "Herb, did you know that biblical law states that a judge who has witnessed a crime is disqualified from acting as a judge in that case?"

"No, I hadn't heard that. But it makes sense."

"Indeed it does. True justice can only be done when the benefit of the doubt can be properly examined. And a person who has witnessed a crime with his own eyes will not be able to objectively examine the defense's case. In your situation, I would like you to think of yourself as the judge who has witnessed the crime. Think of Jennifer as the defendant. My role will be that of the trier of the crime. I intend to help you to objectively examine Jennifer's case."

Dr. Vespa continued. "Our goal, Herb, is to seek a better relationship between you and Jennifer. I have found that the best way to resolve conflict is to first try to reduce the intensity of the negative feelings the parties have toward each other. Now, on a scale of one to a hundred, how intense are your negative feelings toward Jennifer right now?"

"Oh, I would probably say a hundred and fifty."

"OK. Now make believe you were hired as Jennifer's defense attorney in a court of law. How would you describe the reasons behind why she left your marriage?"

I mulled over the question for a few seconds before answering. "Well, reason number one is she claims she doesn't love me. She hasn't admitted to her infidelity, but her actions say otherwise. Her moving to an apartment, her refusing to be with the kids, her wanting to be alone—"

"Stop!" said Dr. Vespa. "Those are all *your* understandings of the breakup. I asked you to be Jennifer's defense attorney. Now, what do you think are her reasons?"

Again, I thought about it for a few moments before I spoke.
"I guess she was unhappy with her life. She found a new companion. She loves her work with the refugees. She didn't feel fulfilled being a wife and mother."

"Good," said Dr. Vespa. "Now, how strongly do you believe your defense arguments are true? Same scale, one to a hundred."

"I get it," I said. "My negative feelings go down when I try to see her side of things. When I look at it selfishly, of course I will be angry and hurt. My pain is very real. But if I take the time to see it her way...Wow. Pretty amazing, Dr. Vespa."

"Herb, let me ask you this. Do you ever think, 'Jennifer stabbed me in the back'?"

"Of course," I said.

"How about, 'Jennifer was not honest with me'?"

"Sure."

"Well, 'stabbing' is an angry and violent word. Of course, we use it as a figure of speech, but don't you think being 'not honest' is a better way to describe her behavior? By changing your feelings, you can reduce your pain. Words are excellent tools when you put them to work to heal."

"I can see how that might be," I said.

"Good. One last thought tonight, and we'll be done. Are you OK so far?"

"Yes, I'm fine. Please proceed," I said.

"Imagine that one day you get a call telling you that your Aunt Mildred, whom you haven't seen since you were very young, is coming to stay with you for a week. It's hard to get excited about hosting someone you know so little about. So you call your mother, who tells you that Aunt Mildred was her favorite cousin growing up. Your mother tells you all sorts of stories about what Mildred meant to her, and how she cared for you when you were young. Your mom even sends you pictures of Aunt Mildred and you playing in the park. Now, suddenly, those warm childhood memories start to flood your mind. How does thinking about your aunt now change your feelings about hosting her for a week?"

"I guess I'd feel more positive about it."

"I'd say you would. And this is what 'gray' thinking is all about. Remember when Jennifer sat in my office and said you were a black-and-white thinker and she was gray?"

"I do."

"Well, by thinking and developing feelings, you can learn to be gray, too."

A Single Parent

———

I WAS SURPRISED TO FIND that time without Jennifer passed quickly. Days I spent at work, solving business problems and dealing with the ever-present needs of my customers and my employees. I loved the challenge my business provided, and I truly enjoyed the people I worked with. Having Dany in my employ made things less complicated at home, too. She came to work and went home as needed.

Dany learned to drive and obtained her driver's license. She began taking the kids to school in the morning and picking them up in the afternoon. She also cooked dinner, did the laundry, cleaned the house, and did anything else that was needed to keep the family together until I came home from work.

As for Jennifer, she was really nowhere in this equation. Now and then she would call to speak with the kids, and sometimes she would meet them for dinner during the week or on weekends. But her contact with the children was sporadic at best. I encouraged Jennifer to explain her absence from their lives and our home. And to do it quickly. From what the children related to me, her rationale for leaving was that she still loved them but needed to live alone for a while. She said, "Daddy is better able to take care of you than I am. He will provide a better life for you than I can."

Well, at least we agreed on something.

———•———

"Shake and shake
The ketchup bottle
First none comes out
And then
A lot'll"
—Bennet Cerf

Ponh called Dany at the office from the payphone in the General Store. The connection wasn't very good, but Dany was expecting his call. She just hadn't known when it would come.

"Dany, when are you coming to Louisiana?"

"I am very busy here at work, Ponh. Besides, Herb needs me to help with the children. I'm not sure when I can come."

"Oh. Can you come next week? Shoe and I have found a boat, and I want to show it to you. And I want you to meet Shoe."

"I will try, Ponh. Let me see what can be done. Call me the day after tomorrow."

"Yes, I will call."

———•———

"Herb, Ponh wants me to visit Louisiana. He wants me to come next week. What do you think? I know we are busy here at work. And can you manage the house and children with me gone?" Dany asked.

I thought for a minute. Things were really easy with Dany around. Why let her leave? Yet, how could I force her to stay? No. That wouldn't be right. It had to be up to her.

"I think you should do what you need to do. If you want to go to Louisiana, you are certainly free to go. Please don't worry about the kids and me. We'll be fine. Of course, you'll be taking Phyda, aren't you?"

"I hadn't thought of that. Yes, of course. Phyda goes wherever I go."

"Just promise me one thing, Dany. Please buy two round-trip bus tickets. You should be able to return home whenever you like." Somehow, I knew they'd return. What I didn't know was when and under what circumstances.

———◆———

Two days later, Ponh called Dany again.

"Hello, Ponh. Phyda and I will leave for Louisiana tomorrow. Please meet us at the bus stop."

"I am so happy, Dany. Can you bring money?"

"Yes. I will bring two thousand dollars. That is all I have now."

Ponh smiled. He would soon buy a boat!

———◆———

I saw Dr. Vespa each Tuesday and Friday night. He would ask me questions, and I would answer him. The appointments always seemed to end too soon. Each visit was magical. By purging my feelings through him, I was gaining personal strength I never realized possible. And I was understanding things about my background—and Jennifer's—that I hadn't before.

For example, my father, Morris, was the second oldest sibling in a family of six children—five boys and one girl. He was born in 1908. When my father was twelve years old, his family's paint business went under. Unable to face failure, my grandfather drowned himself in a quarry. My grandmother was never well after that. My father was forced to drop out of school and find work so that the family could live. So, at age thirteen he went out into the world and got a job.

His very first employer was a company called Lighting Equipment & Supply Company, or LESCO. He was hired to be a store clerk. As fate would have it, there were five people named Morris working at LESCO. (I've often wondered if his name got him the job, but I never dared to ask my father. He was a stern and serious man who demanded respect. I guess I felt it would be disrespectful to find something humorous regarding the family name, even indirectly.) Anyway, his boss asked him if he would mind using the name Harry instead of Morris. Of course, he didn't mind at all. He was just happy to have work. From then on, they called him Harry.

For fifty-two years my father, Morris, also known as Harry, worked at LESCO. He became a well-respected certified lighting consultant and retired at the age of sixty-five, just as he had planned.

But life is never fair. Just as Harry announced his retirement, my beloved mother, Miriam, was diagnosed with lung cancer. She was fifty-seven years old. She never smoked cigarettes herself, but she was around smokers most of her adult life. She loved to play poker. Every week, she would gather at a different friend's home to play. Six or seven women, all chain smokers. Miriam was the only nonsmoker. To the best of my knowledge, she was also the only cancer victim out of all of her smoking friends. I remember when the game came to our house. The stench of cigarette smoke permeated the entire house for days.

I never smoked because of my memories of that smell. My mother died six months after diagnosis.

Another example was Jennifer's adopted father, Hyman. He was born in Russia. Hyman's parents fled the country during the time of the Czars. Hyman, an infant at the time, and his older brother, Max, were hidden in the lining of a large overcoat their mother wore. By some twist of good fortune, they were able to escape Russia. They arrived in America in the early 1900s.

Hyman grew up in Philadelphia, married the bookkeeper at the company where he worked as an accountant, and was a good provider to his family. His one major fault was that he never allowed Jennifer to decide things for herself. Because of this, she grew up totally dependent on him, relying on his judgment about everything.

I resented his domineering treatment of her. His values and mine never quite seemed in agreement. Whenever I confronted Jennifer about this, she listened to me, but she always responded the same way: "I love my dad. He is who he is. Deal with it."

What I later came to realize was that Jennifer had married someone remarkably similar to her father. Yes, I dominated our relationship. I was decisive, a black-and-white thinker. Jennifer went from one strong man, her father, to another, me. It was hard for me to admit it, but Hyman and I had a lot of common traits, many of which were not positive from Jennifer's point of view. In certain ways, I drove her away.

I never would have realized this on my own, but Dr. Vespa got it all out of me.

It was late in December, the sky turned to snow
All round the day was going down slow
Night like a river beginning to flow
I felt the beat of my mind go
Drifting into time passages

Well, the picture is changing
Now you're part of a crowd
They're laughing at something
And the music's loud
A girl comes to you
You once used to know
You reach out your hand
But you're all alone, in these
Time passages.
                              —Al Stewart

Louisiana, Here We Come

———◆———

Dany and Phyda boarded the Greyhound bus bound for Louisiana at exactly the same time and location as Ponh had one month earlier. The only difference was that the weather for their journey was miserable. No sunshine, only rain. Buckets of rain, pounding on the roof of the bus like marbles clattering down on an iron ceiling. Intermittent thunder and lightning compounded the intensity of the noise. Dany and Phyda covered their ears to try to blunt the severity of the racket surrounding them, but they couldn't keep them covered all the time. They chose seats in the middle of the bus. Not that they had much choice. The bus was nearly full when they boarded.

Even though the bus had been parked under an awning during boarding, the violent winds forced the rain everywhere, especially into their bags. The yellow-rubber hooded raincoats they wore kept them partially dry, but their suitcases leaked like sieves. Dany knew the clothes on their backs were it for the entire bus ride. There would be no dry clothes to change into.

———◆———

"Phyda, would you like something to drink?" Dany shouted over the noise.

"Just some water please, Mama."

The bus was about to leave. Its giant windshield wipers swept back and forth with the rhythm of a slow rock song. *"I love rock and roll, so put another dime in the jukebox, baby…"* The diesel engine rumbled as the bus moved forward, and then the hydraulic brakes hissed as they came to a lurching stop. Dany and Phyda fell into the seats behind them. They both screamed cheers of joy as they laughed at being so out of control.

"This is going to be such a fun trip," Phyda said. "How long will it be till we get to Ponh's?"

"Around twenty-four hours, I'd guess. Why don't you ask the driver? With the bad weather and all, it might be longer."

Phyda got out of her seat and walked carefully up the aisle toward the driver. She held on to each seat to balance herself. The bus was now moving quickly.

The bus driver's name was George. The badge on his shirt said so.

She gently tapped his arm twice with her hand. She didn't want to surprise him. "Hi, George. My name is Phyda. Can I ask you a question?"

"Of course you can, little girl. Phyda, is it?"

"Uh-huh. We are going to Louisiana, my mama and me. I would like to know how long will it take."

George smiled while keeping his eyes on the road.

"Hard to tell, Phyda. I'd venture a guess that we'll be there some-time tomorrow morning. Depends on the weather along the way. I was told by the dispatcher in Philly that the storms go as far as Louisiana. But don't worry. I'll get you and your mama there safely. Why don't you just return to your seat and enjoy the ride. We'll be stopping in each state, so you'll be able to get off, have some refreshments, and buy a souvenir or two."

———

The day Dany and Phyda were to arrive, Ponh and Shoe got up early to get the apartment ready. They changed the bed linens, did the laundry, and cleaned the place until it was spotless. Ponh was certain Dany would love Louisiana, and he was determined to make a good early impression.

"Ponh, do you realize that today will be the official beginning of our shrimp business together?" Shoe said. "When Dany brings the two thousand dollars to buy the boat, we will have achieved our dream!"

"Yes, I have been patiently awaiting this day. I am happy to be a fisherman with you, Shoe. I am happy to be marrying Dany. I believe it will be a good day," said Ponh.

"I have an idea, Ponh. Why don't we go down to the dock and give our boat a thorough cleaning inside and out. Let's get her ready to take out when Dany and Phyda come. We can surprise them. I know the weather is not great today, but at least we can make the boat look nice. What do you say?"

"Let's do it," said Ponh.

So Shoe and Ponh drove in Shoe's truck to the dock. By then, the winds were picking up all around them. It appeared that a severe thunderstorm was on the horizon. The sky was darkening and the clouds were thickening. As they were en route, the wind was so strong that Shoe had a hard time holding the truck on the right side of the road. But Shoe was a good driver, and they made it to the dock without being blown off the road. They unloaded the cleaning supplies they'd brought with them and proceeded to the boat, which they had already named DANY.

Shoe volunteered to clean the inside of the boat. He unloaded the supplies in the rain and boarded the boat. He knew he could only clean so much because of the rain, but he was determined to make a good effort. Shoe realized that a hard rain storm is nature's car wash. Wouldn't it be the same with boats as well?

Ponh put on rubber fisherman's waders. They covered his legs up to his waist, and he thought it a good idea to wear them while cleaning the boat in the rain. He enjoyed wearing them. Anything he could do to be a fisherman, he enjoyed. "Here I am," he called to the darkening sky, "Ponh the fisherman! Look at my boots!"

The rain was coming harder now. Ponh thought nothing of it. It was warm and to him it felt calming. He jumped in the water with his brushes and cleaning materials and began to scour the side of the boat. The rain was helpful because as he applied cleaning solution, the rain would be his rinse. Ponh thought, "How wonderful. Nature is helping me clean my boat. This is so very good, and I am at peace."

Then a bolt of lightning and a clap of thunder shouted from the sky, striking Ponh directly on the top of his head. It happened so fast that he could not have felt anything. In a split second, his own flame was instantly extinguished. He was dead.

Shoe saw it happen. After the flash, Ponh fell facedown into the water. He was motionless. There was no blood. Only the smell of burned flesh and hair. The rain pounded the boat and leaped up in splashes from the water around Ponh's floating corpse.

Shoe screamed. "No! Please, no!" He knelt down on the deck of the boat and cried.

It was so sudden, it was stunning. All at once, everything changed. The rain stopped. The wind calmed. The clouds disappeared and the sun shone brightly down upon the earth. The sky transformed into a clear field of blue, so crisp it was hard to imagine it being any other way. It looked so peaceful. And yet, Ponh lay face down in the water beside the boat.

Shoe, shaking and nearly blinded by his tears, jumped off the DANY and landed in four feet of water. He reached out to gather Ponh and carried him to the dock ladder. He climbed the ladder holding Ponh in a fireman's carry and laid him ever so gently on the dock. He then ran to his truck and pulled it close to the dock.

———•———

Pete and Joe ran out of the store when they heard all the honking. They watched as Shoe came roaring up in his truck.

"What's all the commotion about, Shoe?" Joe shouted. "Did you fellas catch a big 'un or somethin'? Where's Ponh?"

"Ponh was hit by lightning. His body is in the back of the truck. I can't believe this has happened. My friend Ponh is gone. We were cleaning the boat. This bolt of lightning came out of nowhere and hit Ponh. He was in the water when it happened. He didn't have a chance."

"Oh, Lord," Joe said.

"The woman he was to marry and her daughter are coming to-day on the bus," Shoe said. "How will I tell them? What can I say?"

"Now try to calm down, Shoe," Joe said. "First, let's get Ponh out of the truck and then get us some help."

Joe was hoping that maybe, just maybe, Ponh was alive and Shoe was mistaken. Of course, he couldn't tell Shoe that. "Why don't I call nine one one and have them take a look at Ponh? They'll know what to do."

Shoe and Pete got Ponh out of the truck and laid him on the wooden bench outside the store. Joe took a look and went to the pay phone and dialed nine one one. An operator answered on the first ring. "Nine one one. What is your emergency?"

Joe responded. "Joe here. We got a man hit by lightning. Appears to be dead. Need help. We're at the Morgan City General Store. Come quick!"

———◆———

While they waited for the ambulance, Shoe began to calm down. He thought of his Buddhist upbringing. Buddha taught him to restrain himself from weeping and wailing in the presence of the departed, no matter how difficult. Shoe knew he was not to upset Ponh's spirit, lest he make it more difficult for his spirit to leave this life. Shoe also must be careful not to suppress his grief by force, ignoring or deny-ing its existence. On the contrary, he was to acknowledge his grief and, through mindfulness and calm reflection, gain self-composure and wisdom. That was the Buddhist way.

The ambulance arrived shortly after the dispatch. The paramedic introduced himself as Billy. After a short but thorough examination, he solemnly confirmed what Shoe already knew to be the case. Ponh was gone.

"How would you like to handle Ponh's remains?" Billy Bob asked. He was very respectful.

Shoe thought for a moment. "I know he has no family," he said. "But a friend of his and her daughter are due to arrive this morning for a visit. I will discuss the situation with her and advise you. Can you take his body to a safe holding area until we decide what to do?"

Billy Bob nodded.

"I'll take Ponh to the morgue. His remains will be held there until you come for him or arrange a funeral. You have my word he will be safe in our custody," said Billy Bob.

Billy Bob wrapped Ponh in a white cotton sheet and then placed him in a large plastic body bag. With Shoe's assistance, he lifted Ponh into the ambulance. Shoe sat in the front seat of the ambulance, and looked out the window as Billy Bob pulled away from the General Store to take Ponh to the morgue.

———

Less than an hour later, the Greyhound from Philadelphia arrived at the Morgan City General Store. Dany and Phyda hopped gingerly off the bus. The warm yet humid air felt good on their still sleep-creased faces. They had awakened several times during the ride, but the patter of the rain and the sounds of the bus lulled them back to sleep. George, the bus driver, had let them sleep through stops along the way. Dany and Phyda were well-rested travelers.

They thanked George as they exited the bus. "Have a good visit you two," he said. Then he drove off, headed north for his next trip.

Dany looked for Ponh but didn't see him. In fact, no one was around. Ponh had told her that he and Shoe would be certain to meet them at the bus stop. Ponh was always prompt. There was a black pickup truck parked in front of the store. No one was in the truck. Maybe Ponh and Shoe were in the store.

Dany and Phyda entered the store. Only Pete stood behind the register. Ponh's description of Pete came to Dany's memory. He had described Pete to her on the phone one day. Heavyset, black, muscles, peaceful, quiet, and content. The look of a holy man. Dany walked up to Pete.

"Are you Pete?"

"Yes, ma'am, I's Pete."

"Have you seen Ponh? Or Shoe? They were to meet my daughter and me here at the bus stop."

"Yes, ma'am. I have seen them. They went with Billy Bob."

"Who is Billy Bob?"

"Billy Bob be the driver. Ambulance."

"Where did they go?"

"To the hospital, I think."

"Was there an accident?"

"Yes, ma'am. There surely was."

"What happened?"

"Lightnin'."

"Lightning? Was someone hit by lightning? Oh no, was it Ponh?"

"Yes, ma'am."

———◆———

SHOE MEETS DANY

Shoe and Billy Bob rolled the body into the county morgue on a gurney. A policeman greeted them as they entered. The morgue was connected to the police station.

"You can bring the deceased in here," he said, pointing to a small room just behind the front desk.

"Hello, Billy. And you must be Shoe. I am Officer Garret, and I will take custody."

Officer Garret was a well-groomed black man who looked to be about twenty-five. His black slacks were pressed and perfectly cuffed atop his gleaming black boots. He wore a white dress shirt open at the collar. His silver police badge and nameplate shone brightly.

Shoe and Billy rolled the gurney into the room indicated by Officer Garret. They lifted the body bag onto a stainless steel table covered with a white cotton sheet. The body bag was heavy and the two men placed it on the table.

"Can you keep my friend here until funeral arrangements are decided?" Shoe asked Officer Garret.

"Yes, I will keep him here. Don't fret, he won't be going any-where," Officer Garret said, trying unsuccessfully to be humorous. He turned to Shoe. "Is it correct that you witnessed the lightning strike?"

Shoe said, "Yes, officer, I did. It was so sudden, so unexpected. There we were preparing and cleaning our boat to show it off to Ponh's friend, Dany, and then *crack*! Ponh was hit. He was in the water when the lightning hit and didn't have a chance. By the time I got to him, his face was in the water, and he wasn't moving. I knew he was dead."

Shoe spoke calmly and slowly to the officer. He was visibly shak-en. Then, all of a sudden he remembered that Ponh had been expect-ing visitors. "Dany and Phyda must have arrived at the bus stop by now. Can I leave to get them?"

"Well, OK, but I'll need to prepare a report. What I'll do is write up your statement as you told it to me. You'll need to come back here to sign it. I'll combine it with Billy's medic's report and turn it over to the coroner. He'll need to examine the body and issue a death certificate after he determines the official cause of death. There shouldn't be a problem. Why don't you return here after you find your friends?"

"Thank you, Officer Garret. Billy, can you drive me to the bus stop, please?"

———

"Herb, this is Dany calling from Louisiana. Can you hear me?" She was using the phone inside the store.

"Like you were in the next room, Dany," I said. "How was your ride? I'd love to hear all about it."

"Maybe later. But…Herb…we…I…I can't find Ponh."

"Phyda and I got off the bus and Ponh was nowhere to be found. A man in the store here told me about an accident involving lightning, and an ambulance and Ponh. I'm worried." Her voice broke. "He's not here, and I don't know what to do. No one else is here to help us and the man I spoke to, his name is Pete, is not very helpful. I think he may not be very smart or something." Dany started to cry.

Herb said, "Dany, try to be calm. I'm sure there's an explanation. Also, come to think of it, didn't Ponh say his friend, Shoe, was to meet you too? What's his story? Do you know?"

"No. Shoe is not here and the man, Pete, could not say where Shoe is either. He said something about a hospital and lightning and Ponh, and…I just don't know."

"Dany, listen. Can you use the telephone to call the police?"

"The police? Why the police? Do you think Ponh did something wrong?"

I realized I had frightened Dany by asking this question.

"No, nothing like that. The police can help you find Ponh. They can assist you."

"Oh. What should I tell them?"

"Just what you told me. I'm certain they'll find Ponh and Shoe. Just try to relax, and I'm sure it will all work out. Call me later after you've found them. OK?"

"I hope so. Thank you, Herb. I will call again later."

———◆———

Dany hung up the phone. Before she could call the police, Billy pulled up with Shoe in the ambulance. Phyda, who was playing outside while Dany was on the phone, saw them first. She ran into the store. "Mommy, some men are here in an ambulance!"

Dany went outside to see. Billy waved and gave them a smile from the driver's seat of the ambulance before hopping out. Shoe got out of the ambulance and slowly walked over to Dany and Phyda, who were standing on the porch in front of the store.

Shoe had not changed his clothing from the morning. His shirt and jeans were covered in red and brown blood from when he'd hauled Ponh's body out of the water.

"Hello. You must be Dany and Phyda. Ponh has told me so much about you. I am Shoe." Shoe held out his hands in friendship.

Dany extended her hands and took Shoe's "Where is Ponh? Is he here? Is he all right? Pete told me something about a hospital and lightning. What is all over your clothes? Is that blood? Why did you come in an ambulance?"

Dany impatiently awaited Shoe's response. Before Shoe could answer, however, she felt herself grow lightheaded. Her eyes rolled back in her head, and she fainted and fell to the ground. Billy ran over to her. He put some smelling salts under her nose, and she awakened immediately. Shoe and Phyda watched her as she sat up. She looked into Shoe's eyes. Shoe spoke.

"Dany, Ponh is dead. I was with him when the accident occurred. We were preparing our boat to show you when a storm came up. Ponh was hit by lightning. He was hit in the head. He did not suffer. He never saw it coming."

Dany reached out to hold Phyda. They hugged each other as they cried quietly. Shoe came over, knelt by Dany's side, and whispered to her.

"Please do not worry. I will care for you and Phyda. Ponh would have wanted me to do so."

Dany lay on her back, stretched out on the sand-and-gravel parking lot. She was in shock. Her heart was pounding, and she felt a pressure building in her head. The feeling was not painful, but it was disquieting.

Her skin was cold, and sweat poured down the sides of her copper-colored cheeks. Her hair was wet and matted from her tears and her sweat and the humidity of Louisiana. The sand stuck to her skin made her feel even more distressed. Her mind was racing. She struggled to get her breathing back to normal. And to stop shaking.

"How can my life be filled with such dynamic twists and turns?" she thought. "I was taught by Buddha to believe that every soul is born into a world of suffering and then is cleansed by practicing right thought, right speech, and right understanding. Haven't I done that? Wasn't my choice to come to be with Ponh in Louisiana right in all these respects? I feel so sad."

More tears came and more thoughts. They came one after the other. And yet it occurred to her that she had hardly known Ponh.

"Was he taken away for a reason? After all, he was unpredictable. Impetuous. Thoughtless, yet caring. Awkward, yet funny. Immature, yet honorable. He had suffered in his life. But he was happy to become a fisherman. And to buy a boat. Why is Ponh gone now? Did I love him? No, not in an intimate sense. I liked him. I felt he was a friend. But he did care deeply for me. He was willing to die by his own hand rather than face losing me."

How ironic. Ponh didn't kill himself. He didn't die by his own hand, yet he lost Dany.

"How will my life change now? I have traveled all this distance. I still have Phyda with me. And now this Cambodian man named Shoe is standing over me. Promising to care for my daughter and me. What is that all about? He certainly befriended Ponh quickly. I have been told that he is a good man, and I believe he is honorable and trustworthy. So I shall not fear his intentions. And then there is Herb and his family, and my responsibilities up north...I need time to sort this all out."

Dany was not alone, but she was scared of the unknown.

———•———

Shoe lifted Dany to her feet. "Please come with me, Dany." Then he took her hand and led her out of the heat and humidity, and into the General Store. Phyda followed them

Dany still felt a little dizzy. Shoe offered to carry Dany, but she refused. So he secured her luggage and pointed to the stairs in the back of the store to his apartment. Dany, steadied by Shoe, climbed slowly, along with Phyda.

Shoe opened the door and begged them to enter. "Please be seated," he said.

"Dany, I hope you and Phyda will be happy here. Ponh was hoping to have us all stay together. Why don't you both make yourselves at home? Please have some water and something to eat from the refrigerator. Shower and change your clothes if you like. I must leave to tend to Ponh's funeral arrangements and sign papers."

Shoe hesitated, coughed a little and then asked Dany, "I know this is hard for you, so sudden and all, but do you have any thoughts about a funeral for Ponh?"

Dany thought for a minute and shook her head. "No," she said. "But I know his body should be handled gently with the greatest love and respect. He was a Buddhist man, and I am certain he died with a pure heart. Please do what you believe to be right, Shoe." Dany's dizziness was beginning to subside. She stood up, walked to the kitchen, and got two glasses of water.

"I promise I will, Dany. I will return here as soon as I am able."

———

Shoe drove quickly to the county morgue. He was anxious to get the paperwork signed and get on to making arrangements for Ponh's funeral. He wondered if Dany knew how to reach Ponh's friends. Would they come to Louisiana to pay their respects?

Shoe was sweating profusely when he arrived. Officer Garret was sitting at attention at the front desk, just as he had been when Shoe saw him for the first time.

"Hello, Shoe. Glad you're here. Were you able to find your visitors?"

"Yes, I was. They were rather upset, not finding Ponh at the bus stop and all. And then not knowing what to do or where to go. Or what happened. They're at my apartment. They know Ponh is dead. Very upset. I left them to get settled while I came to see you. Um, were you able to complete the accident report for me to sign?"

"Yes. I have it right here. Why don't we go into an office to do this?"

Officer Garret led Shoe into a room in the back. Shoe looked all around him. The morgue was eerily quiet. No other police or other staff was anywhere to be found. Shoe wondered where all the people were. "Are you the only one here?" he asked.

"We have a very small budget," Officer Garret said. "Other than the coroner, you're looking at our entire staff. Of course, we have three policemen and a chief, but they are located next to city hall, about half a mile down the road."

"Oh. I guess in a small town, not much happens."

"You got that right, Shoe. Anyway, here is my report, which includes your statement. Are you able to read it?"

"Yes. I can read just fine. I am a high-school graduate. I got my diploma nearly seven years ago." Shoe smiled proudly.

"Well, good for you. Good for you! Please read the entire report. If you agree that it is what you told me, sign it, and I will witness your signature."

Officer Garret handed the report to Shoe. It was only three typed pages long. Shoe took a deep breath and began to read. The report stated the facts exactly as Shoe had told them to Officer Garret. Not one word needed to be changed. Shoe was very relieved. Deep down inside, he had feared that his story might not be believed. Or that he'd be misunderstood. But he had told the truth, and the truth had prevailed!

He signed the report and handed it to the policeman. "Thank you, Officer Garret."

Officer Garret took the signed report from Shoe. "Thank you, Shoe. Oh, for your information, the coroner already examined the body while you were gone. She determined the cause of death to be accidental. Just as you reported. So no further action will be necessary on our part. No autopsy will be required. I can release the body to your custody if you like."

Shoe looked Officer Garret in the eye and with great respect and gratitude. "Do you know of a proper funeral home where I might have my friend Ponh cremated?" he asked. Then he broke down and cried.

———

Shoe returned from the morgue to Dany and Phyda.

"Shoe, I thank you for your kindness and your pledge to care for Phyda and me, but we cannot stay here with you. Or without you." Dany continued to cry as she held Phyda. "You see, my relationship with Ponh was very complicated. He asked me to marry him. He threatened to kill himself if I refused."

"I did not know this, Dany," Shoe said. He shook his head in disbelief. "Ponh never told me. I just assumed you were his wife, and I felt a responsibility to Ponh, and to you and Phyda."

"He never really loved me. I do believe he loved the idea of marrying me. But nothing more. He felt a responsibility to provide for us and chose fishing here in Louisiana. But I never really envisioned myself as a fisherman's wife.

"We slowly became friends, and I traveled to Louisiana to see him as he insisted. I felt I could not turn him down. But he is gone now, and I must raise Phyda as I choose. And I choose to return to Pennsylvania. I am sorry. You seem like a good man, Shoe. I know you mean well. I am glad Ponh had a friend like you."

"What can I do to get you to stay?" Shoe asked.

"Nothing, Shoe. Phyda and I will take the bus home. Perhaps someday we will meet you again under happier circumstances."

———•———

Dany left a message on my answering machine. "This is Dany calling. Phyda and I are coming home on the bus tomorrow. Can you pick us up? Ponh is dead, and I must come home. I hope you will understand. I will call tomorrow before we leave."

Jilly

———◆———

I was determined to get on with my life. Finding new friends seemed like a reasonable way to do this. One of my new friends was Fiameta. She found me.

Fiameta was an artist and a very outgoing woman. She was born in Italy. She'd come to New York as a violin student, gotten a degree in music at Julliard, and married a Chinese doctor. Their marriage lasted less than five years, but it resulted in a lovely daughter, Kim. Kim lived with her father in New York.

Fiameta moved from New York to Philadelphia, where she took a teaching position at Temple University. I literally bumped into her on campus when she just came up to me and introduced herself. I was leaving to get my car after a business meeting. I noticed her coming toward me. She was tall and slender, with long dark hair, green eyes, and an olive complexion. She wore jeans and a revealing red silk blouse. I thought she could have been a movie star.

"Hello. You look like someone I'd like to meet. My name is Fiameta."

"Hi, Fiameta. I'm Herb."

"Herb, you look like a kind yet adventurous soul to me. How would you like to have dinner? With me. At my house. I'll cook, we'll dine and then we'll go together to visit a lady friend of mine. A fortune-teller. What do you think?"

"Do I know you? Is this some sort of a joke or a dream? I've never had an offer like this in my entire life. I honestly don't know what to say."

"No, we don't know one another. But I'm serious. What fun is life without a little surprise now and then? I promise I won't bite, and I'm certain you'll enjoy my company. And when you meet my friend, you'll be grateful. What do you have to lose? Say yes. Come on. Take a chance."

"Well. I'm not sure about this. But OK. Yes."

"Good. Come walk with me. I live two blocks off of Columbia."

I wondered to myself, "Did I just get picked up by a hooker?"

———◆———

I left my car parked on campus, and we walked to Fiameta's house.

"Do you always meet men this way?"

"Why, do you think I'm too forward? I'm Italian, you know. I don't believe in hesitating about anything. I'm hopeful that you get to like me for this trait."

I remained silent as we walked side by side. It seemed like an eternity to me. I felt very unsure and nervous. Then out of nowhere

I courageously said, "When we get to your house, why don't we talk about each other's lives? And when I meet your fortune-teller friend, I can test her to see if she knows her stuff. Sound good?"

"Herb, I think that's a great idea!"

———•———

Fiameta was a wonderful cook. She served a delicious Caesar salad and *al dente* pasta with porcini mushrooms. I opened a bottle of Chianti Riserva and poured two glasses. "*Salute!*" she toasted.

"*Salute!*" I replied.

We finished the meal with homemade tiramisu and fresh-brewed espresso. I hadn't had a home cooked meal like that in a long time.

Over dinner she shared her life story with me. I told her about Jennifer and the children. And about Cambodia.

We smiled at each other, and she asked, "Are you ready for the main event?"

The Chianti had relaxed me. I was ready for anything. I said, "If you mean the fortune-teller, let's go for it."

"Let me call her to let her know we're coming."

———•———

We walked back to campus to get my car. Fiameta didn't have one. "I like to walk everywhere," she said.

I drove to a house ten miles north of campus. The house was located at the top of a hill on a dark street lit by a single streetlight. The only lights coming from inside the house were candles burning in each window. We passed through an ornate iron gate that squealed as I pushed it open. We walked down a long brick path, climbed a couple of steps onto a porch, and went up to a large, double-sized glass door. There was a round iron knocker in the center of the door. I knocked. Not too hard. I didn't want to break the glass.

In less than a minute, an elderly woman came to the door. She was dressed completely in white cotton, which matched her long, straight white hair and her pale-pink complexion. She had the chubbiest of cheeks and a broad smile.

"Good evening, Fiameta and Herb. Did I get that right? I'm so inspired to see you two. Please enter my humble abode. We've got lots to do. So little time. Come on in! My name is Jilly."

We entered the foyer and observed a wide circular stairway. We climbed the stairs to the first landing and Jilly beckoned us into a dark living room filled with red overstuffed sofas. There were three of them, arranged back to back in a triangle, with empty space in the middle. One faced the door, one the window, and one the fireplace. There was no other seating. An odd arrangement. A candle in the window was the only light in the room.

"Please pick a sofa and be seated," Jilly said. She sat on the sofa facing the fireplace.

Fiameta chose to sit on the sofa facing the front window. I chose to sit next to Fiameta. The sofa facing the door remained empty.

"Very predictable, you two," said Jilly.

"How so?" I asked.

Jilly said, "Well, I know the two of you just met. But you had dinner and wine together, right?"

I smiled. "Yes, that's right. But what does that have to do with our choice of seating?"

"It tells me that, at some level, you have bonded with each other. You, Herb, felt secure enough to sit next to Fiameta in a candlelit room, when you could just as easily have sat next to me or on the other sofa. But you didn't. Why?"

"I have no idea," I said.

"Fiameta, did you tell Herb anything about me?" Jilly asked.

"Only that you are a good friend and that you are a fortune-teller."

"Jilly, why don't you just talk about fortune-telling?" Fiameta suggested.

"I would be pleased to. First, let me tell you, Herb, that I am eighty-three years young. I have been practicing palmistry nearly all my life. Palmistry is the art of characterization and foretelling the future through the study of the palm. It is also known as chirology."

"So, you're really not a fortune-teller, you're a palm reader?" I asked.

"Yes and no. You see, I have been trained to interpret the various lines and palmar features in a person's hand. These lines and features give me suggestions or messages, and tell me about the person's past, present, and future. I guess you might say the product of my efforts is a fortune- or a future-telling of events. Fiameta, why don't you tell Herb why he is here tonight?"

"Do you really want me to tell?"

"Yes. I believe he is entitled to know."

"OK," said Fiameta. "Herb, Jilly read my palm last week. You see, not only is she a palmist, she is teaching chirology at Temple University, and I am a student taking her course in addition to teaching music. You, Herb, are sort of my homework assignment. Sorry if I got you here under unusual circumstances. But you did come willingly, right?"

I nodded. "Of course I did. Yes."

"You see, when Jilly read my palm, she saw certain elements or temperaments that suggested someone new would enter my life. My assignment was to find you."

I stood up, turned away from Fiameta, and faced toward Jilly. "Wow. Jilly, I am very impressed. Do you really think I'm that 'someone new' in Fiameta's life?" I asked.

"You're here, aren't you?" said Jilly. "And as I said before, the two of you have bonded."

I felt chills run down my spine. So much for my fantasies about that hooker thing. Disappointed? Oh yeah! Feelings? Somewhat relieved. There was no money involved as far as I could tell. I didn't think these characters were grifters. I was very happy to be Fiameta's friend.

"Herb," Jilly said, "how would you like to take a cram course in palmistry? By agreeing, I think you will gain an understanding of why you are here with Fiameta and perhaps gain an understanding about your own life as well."

"I'd be most happy to take your course, Jilly."

"Wonderful," said Jilly.

"I'm very pleased you've agreed, Herb," said Fiameta.

"OK. Then let's leave this room and climb some more stairs," said Jilly.

Up we went. Jilly led, gingerly taking two stairs at a time. Her white cotton garb flowed in rhythm with her strides, and she appeared almost nymphlike. Fiameta followed, and I brought up the rear. Neither of us had Jilly's energy. We were both winded from the sprint up the stairs.

We reached the landing and entered a room without windows or a door. It was painted dark navy blue and was lit by ten candles placed strategically on the floor against one wall. A variety of silver moons and stars seemed to reflect the candlelight and glisten against the blue walls. As we entered the room, I felt as if I were entering an otherworldly place. It seemed very calming. In the middle of the room there was a narrow table, about a foot and a half wide. The table was covered with a white silk sheet. Two white padded chairs were placed on one side of the table and a third chair was on the opposite side. Jilly asked Fiameta to sit next to her, and I sat opposite Jilly.

"Let us begin," said Jilly. She spoke very softly and slowly. "We are in a very serene and spiritual place. Only very unique people are permitted here. I deem the two of you special. Please listen as I speak. You may ask questions when I have completed my lesson. Until then, please remain silent." She went on, "Palmistry originated in the Far East. It has been used in the cultures of India, Tibet, China, and Persia. Many ancient communities including Hindus, Hebrews, Greeks, Romans and others have also practiced it. However, it is more important for you to understand what Palmistry is than where it was used or who used it.

"Palmistry is the practice of elevating a person's character or future life by reading the palm of that person's hand. In ancient times, it was believed that one's destiny is formed only once. The ancients believed that the hands did not change over time and that one reading was sufficient. Today, we know that hands change over time as a result of events in one's life. When a reading occurs may determine the knowledge gained from that reading. Timing is very important.

"Now, let's get down to some basics. Oh, and please relax, Herb. I see you are growing tense. We can enjoy and learn better if we maybe add a little humor? Did you realize that we have two hands? Of course you do. The left hand and the right hand. There, that was fun, wasn't it? Don't answer, just listen." I chuckled.

"Which hand should we read?" Jilly continued. "The left hand is the one we are born with. It does not change. The right hand is what we have and will have made of our life. The past is the left; the future is shown in the right. The left is what the gods give you; the right is what you do with it. The right is read for right-handed people, while the left is read for left-handed people. And so on and so on."

"Do you believe any of what I just said?" Jilly asked. "You can answer this question, Herb."

"I have no idea, Jilly. I suppose don't know if it's all true. If I am going to believe a fortune-teller, I think there should be proven theories upon which to rely. I never met a chirologist before, and I plead total ignorance about this subject. But I am eager to learn. I guess it makes some sense," I said.

"Well," Jilly said, "let's just say some of it might be true, and some of it might not be true. I believe it is up to the instinct and experience of the practitioner. Well, I think we've gone pretty far. Any questions, Herb?"

I shook my head.

"Would you like me to read your palms, Herb?" Jilly asked.

"Tonight? Right now? Yes, Jilly, I would like that very much. But I have a question. If you say no, I will understand. But if you say yes, I will be overjoyed!"

"Now I am curious," Jilly said.

"First, my friends are never going to believe what has happened this evening. I hope to introduce Fiameta to them, but is there any way I can have you make a tape of my first fortune-telling experience? Do you ever do anything like that? I have a tape recorder in my car, and I would really appreciate it if I could tape your words. What do you think?"

Jilly agreed without hesitation. "In all my days, no one has requested such a thing. But for you, Herb, the answer is yes."

I ran down the stairs, got the tape recorder, and returned to the dark-blue room with silver moons and stars glittering on the walls.

This time, the trip up the stairs was not too bad. I was pumped and excited to get my fortune told. Hopefully, I thought, I will get a good one. After all, I was due for some good news.

I plugged the recorder in, set it up on the white silk table, and took my place opposite Jilly and waited for her to begin.

"Please turn it on," said Jilly. "Are you ready?"

"I am."

"It is eighteen minutes past nine on Monday, August eighteenth. The year is 1982. I am with Herb and Fiameta. I am about to begin reading Herb's palm. He has agreed to allow Fiameta to be here as a witness. Herb, will you please place both of your hands palms down on the table before me?"

"Palms down? I thought you would want my palms up."

Jilly gave me a look.

"Whoops. Sorry. I know, no questions."

"Before I read your palms, I must examine the shape of your hands. Hand shape discloses character traits. The color and texture of the skin and fingernails, the prominence of the knuckles—all are signals to the palmist."

"Do you know what the Four Elements in nature are?" Jilly asked me. "Everyone reflects them in their hands. Fiameta, why don't you answer? While you're at it, why don't you explain to Herb what these elements are all about?"

Fiameta took a deep breath and looked me deeply in the eyes. I could feel her intensity.

"The Four Elements are earth, air, water, and fire. Palmists classify hands into these four categories. Earth hands have broad, square palms and fingers, thick or coarse skin, and ruddy color. Air hands have square or rectangular palms with long fingers, protruding knuckles, low-set thumbs, and dry skin. Water hands appear as oval-shaped palms with long, flexible fingers. And finally, fire hands have flushed skin and shorter fingers. Their palms are angular, either square shaped or rectangular."

"Thank you, Fiameta. Now, Herb, I'd like you to turn your hands palms up."

"May I please stretch first? I'm not used to holding my hands in one place for such a long time," I said.

"Of course."

I removed my hands from the table, clasped them together with my fingers intertwined, and cracked my knuckles. Jilly and Fiameta both laughed loudly. Then I stood up, raised my arms, and stretched.

I let out a huge sigh. Then I sat back down at the table. All the while the tape recorder was running.

A Difficult Reading

"OK. Let's begin. Since we are recording this, I will attempt to go slowly," said Jilly.

"Herb, by examining your hands palms down, I have determined that you have Air hands. This type of hand tends to have more lines with less clear definition than the other types. Your hands tell me that you are a very complex individual. By the way, you have come to the right place, because I am a very capable palmist. I specialize in difficult readings."

"Thank you, Fiameta. Without you, I would never would have met Jilly." Fiameta nodded and whispered for me to be silent.

"I am now studying your lines, Herb," Jilly said. "The three most important lines on your palms are called Heart, Head, and Life. Can you venture a guess as to what they might mean?"

"All right," I said. "The Heart line has to do with love. The Head line has to do with intelligence. And the Life line has to do with health. Am I close?"

"Very close!" Jilly exclaimed.

"The Heart line is found toward the top of your palm, right under the fingers. It defines your emotional living. It indicates romantic perspectives and intimate relationships. I see that you are beginning anew in your life. You are in the painful process of divorcing and are beginning to heal. All signs indicate that you will find another.

I sense the aura of fresh-baked bread around you. Soon it will influence your life."

"Fresh-baked bread? How can you see bread in my palms?" I asked.

"Not *see* bread. Sense the aura of fresh-baked bread. There is a big difference," Jilly said. "Have you ever smelled fresh-baked bread just coming out of the oven? It's one of the most appealing and sensual odors you'll ever smell."

"No, I haven't. You won't believe this, but I honestly haven't smelled fresh-baked bread before. But I'm sure looking forward to it," I said.

"Very well. Let's continue. The Head line begins at the edge of your palm, under your index finger, and passes toward the outer edge of your palm. I can tell that you are both creative and analytical from this line. You have a strong thirst for knowledge and are highly intelligent. You have a great appreciation for people and are well liked by everyone. But you tend to be very trusting, and this gets you in trouble sometimes."

"How so?" I asked.

"Think about it, Herb. It was not so long ago your wife betrayed your trust, did she not?" said Jilly.

"Oh yeah." I nearly forgot. Whoops. "How did you know that?"

"Actually," Jilly said, "your forgetting is a good sign. It is perfectly normal to mentally block painful events in our lives. As our hands change, our lines heal and change, too."

"The Life line extends from the edge of the palm above the thumb and arcs toward the wrist. This line reflects physical health and general well-being. Often the Life line and the Head line are joined together. I see that you will enjoy a long life with mainly good health. This is all I see tonight."

"Thanks, Jilly. But what about Fiameta? Aren't you going to tell me how she fits into my life?" I asked.

"That is between the two of you. I will not be commenting about that this evening." She then stood up abruptly and bid us good-bye by motioning us to leave.

"But Jilly," I said, "why won't you comment? I am very disappointed with your answer. Actually, I feel you are not telling us something we might need to know. Why?"

No answer from Jilly. Just silence.

As quickly as Jilly's demeanor had shifted, so had mine. Annoyed and disappointed, I packed up my tape recorder and marched down the stairs. Fiameta followed. Neither of us spoke as we left the house. We took care to lock the glass door behind us after we'd let ourselves out.

———◆———

We walked to the car, and I opened the passenger-side door for Fiameta. She got in, and I closed her door. I went around the back of the car—I never go around the front—to the driver's side. I got in.

"Fiameta, can you tell me what just happened?"

"I will try, but I, too, am confused. Jilly can be quite eccentric. I am guessing she slipped into one of her moods where drama and mystery reside. I appreciate it that you asked about us. I was wondering myself. She is challenging us to figure out our own answers. I guess we have our work cut out for us. I'm game if you are."

Some Enchanted Evening

IT WAS A CHILLY WEDNESDAY evening in early September. A neighborhood friend, another single parent, Susan, had encouraged me to get out of the house and to begin to meet people. We'd been friends for many years, having raised our children in the same neighborhood. She was well aware of my situation with Jennifer. I knew she wanted to date me, but I liked her only as a friend, and I told her so.

Even so, Susan was persistent. She invited me to our local temple, Torah Ami. There was a group meeting there for single parents. Susan suggested that I might enjoy meeting other people in my situation. I agreed to go with her, though I had minimal expectations of having a good time.

Torah Ami was located just a few blocks from Surrey Road, so Susan and I went together in my car.

I had reservations about this whole singles thing, and on the way to the temple I shared them with Susan. "I'm not sure whether I can meet new people just yet," I told her.

"Try to relax, Herb," Susan said. "Just be yourself. You'll be fine."

When we entered, the meeting was about to begin. I quickly checked out the room. It was a well-lit school classroom. The adults looked kind of funny seated at the small desks. I knew no one there.

A tallish woman with short brown hair went up to the front of the room and stood before the teacher's desk.

Beth began, "For those of you who don't know me, my name is Beth Sherman. If my name strikes you as familiar, that's because my husband is Rabbi Sherman. First, let me welcome all of you. If you are a single parent, you've come to the right place. At the request of several of our members, I decided to facilitate the formation of this group. Once we have gotten organized and acquainted, I intend to hand the leadership of this group over to one of you after, as would be appropriate.

"The name of our group is Options. Its purpose is to provide a forum for single parents to share their experiences with one another. As we get to know one another better, my hope is that everyone will benefit greatly from taking part in the group. Obviously, all our discussions will be treated confidentially.

"For those of you here for the first time—and I see a few new faces—why don't we start with introductions. Please state your name and anything you'd like us to know about your present situation. Herb, why don't you start?"

To my utter amazement, there were only two men in the room. I began to rise to speak, but the other gentleman in the room stood first. "My name is Herb, and I am a single parent with two sons. I have been divorced for a little over a year. Thank you."

You could have knocked me off my chair! What were the odds of two Herbs in one single parents meeting? Herb sat down and it looked like I was next. I stood up.

"You ladies and, gentleman, Herb, are not going to believe this, but my name is Herb."

"Hi, Herb!" they all exclaimed. Everyone had a good laugh. I laughed along with them.

"I'd like to thank Susan for inviting me," I continued. "I am separated from my wife of over twelve years. We are in the process of getting a divorce. I have three children, two boys and a girl. They live with me. Right now, I have sole custody. I know nothing about single parenting, but I believe my challenges are just beginning. I hope I can learn from you all by belonging to this group."

After I finished speaking, there was a rumbling of conversation in the room. Beth called order and then, one at a time, the remaining singles (all women) in the room stood, identified themselves, and disclosed their marital status. Most were divorced. Two were widows.

One woman in particular caught my attention. She stood at her desk near the front of the classroom. She was tall and slender, with curly blond hair and a peaches-and-cream complexion. Her smile seemed to light up the room. I found her very attractive.

"My name is Andi. I am divorced and have been a single parent for over eight years. I have one son, Scott, who is the light of my life. I helped form this group because I believe we single parents are growing in numbers, and we lack clarity in many areas about single parenthood. I am chairman of the Awareness Committee. I encourage you to join me in our effort to inform others."

I thought, "I want to be on Andi's committee!"

After the introductions, several committees were formed, and we all exchanged our contact information. I joined two committees: the Awareness Committee, chaired by Andi, and the Political Action Committee, chaired by a young widow named Sandra. Her husband had been a state representative. She believed his contacts could be helpful from a political perspective.

We all agreed to meet again next Wednesday and the meeting was adjourned. I looked around for Andi, but she was already gone. So I went up to Sandra and told her I looked forward to working with her. I waited for Susan to finish talking with some of the other group members. Then I drove her home.

———◆———

As soon as I got back to the house, I dialed Andi's phone number. She answered on the fourth ring.

"Hello."

"Andi, this is Herb. We sort of met, but not formally, at Torah Ami tonight. Just so you're not confused, I'm the second Herb, the one with three kids. Is it convenient to talk now?"

"Yes, I just got home. I'm relaxing in front of the TV. My son, Scott, is already in bed. I'm free to talk for a bit. I'm really glad you called, Herb."

"Thanks. I looked for you after the meeting. I was hoping to maybe get some coffee, but you'd already left."

"Well, it's just that I don't like leaving Scott alone at night. My next-door neighbors are there, and he knows to go to them if he needs anything, but he's only ten, so I wanted to get home promptly."

"I understand. I feel the same way. Don't like to leave the children alone. My kids are being watched by Dany, a Cambodian refugee who lives in our home with her daughter, Phyda.

"Anyway, would you like to have dinner this Friday night? You can pick the time and place. That is, if you're not busy. What do you say?"

"I'd like that."

"Yes. I mean, I'm not busy. I'd need to get a sitter, but that shouldn't be a problem. I work downtown, so how about picking me up at seven thirty? Do you know where I live?"

"I've got your address. I'll call you for directions tomorrow night. One last thing—where would you like to go?"

"Do you like barbecued ribs, Herb? There's this place in Jenkintown called The Rib Rack. They have great ribs! And their coleslaw is to die for."

"I've never been there, but yes, I do love ribs. I'll make a reservation."

"Good. Call me tomorrow to confirm, OK?"

"Sure thing. Talk to you tomorrow, Andi. Good night."

———•———

After I hung up, I felt like a teenager who'd just scored a date with a really hot babe. It was quite a jolt to feel that way at thirty-nine years old. I guessed Andi to be around thirty-four, but I couldn't be certain. My excitement notwithstanding, we weren't kids. Not even close. We both were single parents, although I was much newer to it than Andi. She'd been single for eight years. I wondered what that must be like. Lonely? Fun? Definitely challenging.

I retired for the night thinking about my life, how things were changing before my eyes.

———•———

I called Andi Thursday night to confirm our dinner date. I'd made an eight o'clock reservation at the Rib Rack, so I'd pick her up at seven thirty. She gave me precise directions, including where to park near her apartment. We chatted for a little while about our busy day, my crazy customers, and her crazy tenants (she was a property manager). And then we said good night.

———•———

I got home early from the office on Friday. I took a long hot shower and put on my favorite blue turtleneck shirt, black shoes and slacks, and topped it all off with my Armani leather jacket. Black, of course. Friday evening was here, and I was ready for my date with Andi. I even got my car washed for the occasion. And what a car it was: a 1982 Chevy Citation, cream and orange.

I followed Andi's instructions and parked a few spots over from where she'd advised. Her chosen spot for me was taken. She lived in a condominium called Beaver Hill. There were three buildings, North, South, and West. She lived on the first floor in the South building. With the help of a courteous, liveried doorman named Carlton, I found my way to her apartment.

I walked down a long hallway and stopped outside her door. My heart was racing and my brow was sweating. Why was I so anxious? I was just calling on a new friend to take to dinner.

I rang the bell. Andi opened the door. She smiled. "Hi, Herb. You look nice. Right on time." She welcomed me into her home. She was even prettier than I remembered. She asked me to sit on the sofa in the living room. She offered me a glass of wine. We toasted to our evening together.

And then I noticed a smell, something special. Something sensual. "Andi. Are you baking fresh bread in the kitchen?"

"Yes, as a matter of fact, I am. For some reason I can't explain, I decided to bake a challah when I got home from work tonight. Smells pretty good, doesn't it?"

"Andi, you are not going to believe what I am about to tell you, but here goes…"

———————

The sitter, sixteen-year-old Katie, arrived around a quarter to eight, just as Andi and I had finished our wine. She lived in the same building, two floors up. Andi introduced me to Katie. Scott came out of his room just then, but he wasn't very talkative.

"Anyhow, guys, we're going out to dinner not too far away, so we'll be back fairly early," Andi said. "The number of the restaurant is on the fridge if you need me."

"Scott will be fine," Katie said. "Not to worry. Where are you going?"

"Rib Rack. Do you know it?"

"I've never eaten there, but I've heard they have awesome ribs."

Scott was very fond of Katie. "Bye, Ma," he said as he and Katie went off to play in his room, leaving Andi and me alone.

"Do you need a coat, Andi?" I asked. "It's rather chilly for September."

Andi got a jacket from the hall closet. I helped her put it on. Its gold color complemented her curly blond hair and her vivid blue eyes.

We walked to the stairs, said good night to Carlton at the door, and walked to my car. I opened the door for Andi.

"Thanks, Herb." She smiled. I smiled back.

Srey

Srey stood about five feet tall. She was stylishly dressed in fine European clothing and shoes. Her black hair, large eyes, and olive skin were evidence of her Cambodian heritage. The strength of her persona was reflected in her posture and her smile. She appeared to be a woman of sophistication and means.

Srey was the wife of a wealthy and powerful real estate investor living in Phnom Penh, Cambodia. While her husband tended to his business and political affairs at home, she was privileged to travel throughout the world. The refugee problem and the war that created the horrendous conditions in her country seemed not to affect her ability to do as she pleased. Money was no object. She was determined to make a difference with her life.

Her health was poor, though you'd never guess it from her appearance. She traveled to Philadelphia to seek medical care. Srey knew many physicians at the University Hospital.

Srey sought a specialist in blood diseases. She believed she was suffering from leukemia and felt the care and treatment in the United States would be better than any she could find elsewhere.

After finishing up at the hospital, Srey paid a visit to the office of the Children's Family Service of the Lutheran Church, where she met with Jennifer.

Instead of a desk and chair, Jennifer had furnished her office with a round table and six chairs. Files were stacked neatly in piles on the floor at the back of the office. The telephone hung on the wall, reachable from the table but out of the way. Numerous photos of Cambodian children adorned the walls.

"Please have a seat, Srey. Would you like tea or something else to drink?"

"Tea would be fine. With a little milk, please."

Jennifer dialed her secretary and requested two teas, one with milk and one with lemon.

"Srey," Jennifer began, "In my short time here at Lutheran, I have learned that much needs to be done for the people of Cambodia. So much, in fact, that it often seems impossible. An entire educated class of people has been eliminated from your country by the atrocities of the Khmer Rouge. Because of this, the refugees coming to the United States are mostly without skills or education.

"My primary job here is to help refugees obtain the training and language skills that will enable them to find work. I know Lutheran has limited funds, and I realize that my job could be eliminated at any time. What will happen to the refugees that come after I am gone? Surely, things will be more difficult for them. To my knowledge, there aren't many programs such as Lutheran's. With your contacts in Cambodia and your help and guidance, I want to try something new.

"I would like to travel to Cambodia. I would like to live in Cambodia. I plan to start a small business exporting goods made in Cambodia, and distributing them in America. I would provide training for the people I hire. I can afford to travel back and forth to the States as needed. My American staff would be made up of refugees. Needless to say, my staff in Cambodia would be Cambodian as well. In addition, I want to locate an orphanage."

"An orphanage? Why an orphanage?" asked Srey.

"You need to understand, I was adopted as an infant." Jennifer began to cry. "I was blessed to have adopted parents who loved me. I want to give that to Cambodian children too.

"I want to fund a foundation so money can begin to flow to the orphanage from America. The money would be used to care for the babies and begin to create international adoption procedures to help find them better lives. That's it. What do you think?" Jennifer said as tears sprinkled down her cheeks. She took a tissue from the box on the table and patted her cheeks dry.

"I think it is most interesting plan," Srey said. "You are a very ambitious woman, Jennifer. Let me ask you a few questions. Are you aware that I have knowledge of your relationship with Tola? I wonder if he is suggesting these ideas to you. I know he is a most persuasive and charming young man. Have you given thought to your children? How will they feel about your moving to Cambodia? How do you know if you will even like being there? I am not trying to discourage you. I am just very surprised that you have such an aggressive agenda. How will the Lutheran organization react to your plan?

I Wish I Knew Then What I Know Now

OVER TIME, MY ANGER AND contempt for Jennifer subsided. I became used to being a single parent and, for the most part, Jennifer stayed out of my life.

Then one day she telephoned me.

"Herb, I would like a divorce. I have retained a lawyer and will be filing papers very soon. I hope you will not fight me on this. I want to get on with my new life."

Just that simple. Just that cold. Just like that. Over the telephone, no less. Her words landed on my head like a ton of bricks. I had been counseled to expect I'd get such a call from her eventually, though I'd had no idea when it would come. As much as I'd tried to prepare myself for it, it hurt.

I could feel my blood pressure rising. I began to tremble and my hands felt clammy. What should I say?

I responded as calmly as I could. Under the circumstances, it took a great deal of effort for me to do so. I took a deep breath.

"I understand, Jennifer...I don't want to fight. I will get counsel of my own and try to make this as painless as possible for both of us. I want the children to be spared any unnecessary grief. Will you agree to work with me to do that?"

"Yes," Jennifer said. "I will agree to whatever you deem fair. But I would like to have joint custody of the children. I will be away most of the time, but I would like a reasonable amount of time to see them when I am able to do so."

I knew what that meant. Jennifer was planning to live in Cambodia with Tola. She probably wouldn't be around much anyway.

"I will need to talk to my attorney, but I think that shouldn't be a problem."

We both lived up to our promise of no fighting, and the children were not made to suffer at all. Nearly fourteen years of marriage, over.

———

Jennifer and Tola married in a Buddhist Temple in downtown Philadelphia. They bought a small ranch house several miles from Surrey Road in a different school district, and the children visited on weekends as we'd agreed in the divorce. This gave me some time alone to rebuild my personal life.

Srey found Jennifer and Tola a first-floor apartment in a secure compound for international residents in Phnom Penh, Cambodia. Srey casually mentioned to Jennifer that she and her husband owned the building.

Lutheran permitted Jennifer to reduce her hours, and granted her leaves of absence to travel to Cambodia to prepare for her ultimately moving there.

Jennifer's vision to live and work in Cambodia was becoming a reality. But soon after arriving in Cambodia for the first time, there was an issue that Jennifer had never expected.

One night after dinner, Tola and Jennifer were drinking wine together. It was a very warm and humid evening, and the candles' flames were still in the windless air.

"A beautiful night, isn't it?" Tola said. He sat close to Jennifer and held her hand.

"Yes, it is beautiful, Tola. I have never been so happy. It's incredible to me how my life has changed so quickly."

She looked into his eyes and smiled. He looked away.

"Is there something wrong, Tola? Why did you look away just now?" Her face reddened and perspiration broke out on her forehead and began to drip in her eyes and burn.

"Jennifer. There is something I need to tell you. Something I should have told you months ago but didn't. Now I feel I must."

"What is it, Tola? Please tell me what it is."

"I have a son. An American son. He lives in Philadelphia with his mother."

Boys Will Be Boys

It was springtime, March 1984.

Andi and I were in love. We alternated between staying in her apartment and at my house. My children lived with me. Andi's son, Scott lived with Andi. Commuting back and forth between the two residences, dealing with different schools and multiple activity schedules, made for a hectic lifestyle for all of us.

We wanted all our kids to be together under one roof, so we decided to blend our families. We planned to marry in April. We purchased a five-bedroom house with a swimming pool on Parkview Road in Cheltenham. Only Scott would need to change schools, but we felt this would be the best move for everyone. The school change was the only negative. The house was perfect for us. There were many young children in the neighborhood.

Closing on the house went smoothly. The move was scheduled for the next day. Since the kids were in class during the closing, Andi and I picked them up after school to give them their first look at their new house.

We piled into my Citation. The boys stuffed themselves in the tiny backseat, while Molly sat on Andi's lap in front. The new house was just a few blocks from Molly's school.

Andi and I were very excited. The kids, well, not so much.

"Why do we have to move?" said Greg, now fourteen. Drew was twelve, Scott was eleven, and Molly was eight.

"Yeah, why do we, Dad?" Drew said.

"I don't know about this, Ma," Scott said.

Andi smiled. Actually, she glowed. We were prepared for this.

"Well, guys, you know that we are becoming a family, and families normally live together under one roof, in one home. Right now, we live in two," said Andi. "Herb and I know you're going to love it here."

"Besides, you're already friends with some of the neighbors," I added.

"How about we give it a try? Why don't we go inside, check it out, and choose our new rooms."

"Well, OK," said Drew. The others assented as well.

We drove into the driveway located on the right side of the split-level house. The sign on the lawn said SOLD.

Our new house seemed to beckon us inside. Its curb appeal was irresistible. The property was freshly manicured and the driveway freshly sealed. The sun rays shone through the tall trees onto the brown-shingled roof and newly washed white siding. The open gate at the back of the driveway revealed the crystal-clear water in the swimming pool. The scent of dogwood blossoms and fresh-cut grass filled the air.

I pulled into the driveway and cut the engine. The children all squirmed their way out of the car and dashed to the pool.

"Can we go swimming now?" Molly asked. Never mind that she hadn't brought a bathing suit.

"Sorry," I said. "We are only here today to see the house and pick our rooms, and make sure we are ready for the movers tomorrow. There will be plenty of time to swim later on. Don't you worry." Turning to Andi, I suggested that we all go to the front door and enter our new home together. The kids all ran out the pool gate, across the lawn to the front door of the house. Andi and I followed. She had the key.

She unlocked the door and opened it. Everyone walked gingerly into the foyer and then into the living room. The house was completely empty. The previous owners had removed all their possessions and left us a clean empty house.

The children's reactions were brief and to the point.

"Wow! This house is awesome," said Greg.

"Looks like an empty museum to me," said Drew.

"Sweet," said Scott.

"I love it!" said Molly.

Andi assumed the role of tour guide. "This house is called a split-level. We entered the house through the foyer, and we are now standing in the living room."

"I knew that," said Greg. "I'll bet the next room is the dining room."

Andi replied, "You are correct, sir!" Everyone laughed.

Drew chimed in. "And next to the dining room is the kitchen. I see the fridge and the stove."

"Very good, Drew," Andi said. Drew smiled. She continued, "In the kitchen is a door leading to the back of the house, where the deck, barbecue, and pool are located. Next to the kitchen is a den where we can watch TV and play games."

By now, everyone was blown away. And they hadn't even seen the rest of the house yet. Andi told them, "The bedrooms are all on the upper level. There are five of them. One for Herb and me, and one for each of you. There are two bathrooms upstairs. You guys will get to share your own bathroom."

Molly chimed in. "Can't I have my own bathroom? I don't want to share with those boys. Yuck!"

"Molly, I'm afraid you'll just have to learn to share."

We all ran up the steps to the upper level.

The time had come for me to make the big announcement. "All right, everyone. You guys can pick your bedrooms now. The one in the back is for Andi and me. All the others, three on this level and one upstairs, are up for grabs. It's up to you. They are pretty much all the same size. It just depends which one you like. Molly, since you are the youngest, why don't you start?"

Andi and I held our collective breaths. I smiled at her. I looked around at all the kids. I expected conflict, disagreement from the boys. But...

Not a word from anyone.

"I want this one," shouted Molly as she jumped up and down with glee. She chose the room in the front of the house on the left. She ran into it and plopped down on the floor.

"OK," I said. "Good choice, Molly. Now, Scott, it's your turn."

Greg spoke up before Scott could choose.

"Dad. Since I'm the oldest, I think I should choose next."

I thought this might happen. But I decided to let it play out. "Scott," I asked, "are you all right with Greg choosing next?"

"Depends which room he wants," Scott said. "I want the room in the front next to Molly. If Greg wants that room, I will be unhappy." He appeared very serious.

"Greg, what do you think?" I asked.

Greg looked at Scott and said, "Dude, you've got your room. I want the penthouse room on the next level. If that's OK with Drew, then we're done."

Drew said, "No problem. It's fine by me. I wanted to be next to Scott anyway."

———◆———

Our plan was to move into our new home the next day.

We ordered groceries by phone for morning delivery from the local market. The new bedroom furniture and kitchen table and chairs were to be delivered in the morning.

Move-in day was to consist of packing personal items from Andi's apartment and our stuff from Surrey Road, and hauling it over to the new house while the kids were in school. All the other furniture would come later. Andi was working with a decorator and her selections would take additional time to deliver.

The day went quickly. All the deliveries arrived on time in good condition. The furniture fit perfectly. Andi and I made the beds and put away the groceries.

Next, we drove to pick up a U-Haul truck. Surrey Road was first and Andi's apartment second. At each location, we packed up all our personal items. We brought them into the new house and placed them in their proper locations. Then we returned the truck.

We were exhausted.

"Well," I said to Andi, "I think we're done. Wasn't too bad, was it?" I embraced her as we looked into each other's eyes.

"Not too bad," she said. "But our adventure is just beginning. Our kids are great, and we bring a lot of love to this new home. I'm optimistic. How are you feeling?"

"Excited. I love our new family, and I love you. And I love our new house. I'm feeling very good, thank you."

———◆———

We picked everyone up at school and went to an early dinner at Rizzo's. Pizza, eggplant parm sandwiches, cheese steaks, hoagies. The best in Philly!

After dinner, Scott wanted to see his old home one last time. We all went in and sadly said our good-byes to apartment A-20. It was dark by the time we got to Parkview Road.

Everyone piled out of the car and entered the house. We turned on the lights, and the first thing the kids saw was the new pink barn-board kitchen table, surrounded by six chairs upholstered in pink leather. Without commenting on the color, which I expected from the boys, they ran up the stairs to their rooms.

Shouts came from every room. "I love my new room! I love my new bed! The furniture is awesome!"

"How did you know I would like it? But I do! Are we really going to sleep here tonight?"

"First, homework," Andi called up the stairs, "then sleep. We are here forever. This is our family's new home."

"Lights out at nine o'clock. We'll come to tuck you in if you like."

Nine o'clock came. Andi and I kissed each of the boys good night. Molly wanted Andi to read her a story. She did.

Afterward, I came to tuck her in, and Andi and I retired to our bedroom. I knew the minute our heads hit the pillow, we would be asleep. That is exactly what happened.

Two hours later, the doorbell rang. We both awoke with a start.

"Who could possibly be ringing our doorbell at eleven thirty at night?" I said.

I put on my robe and went downstairs. I looked out the peephole and saw a man standing there. He was wearing a suit and tie, and he looked tired. I opened the door, and he gave me a weak smile, but I could sense he had not come by for a friendly chat.

"Hi, Herb. I'm Barry Aver, from next door. I suppose I should have welcomed you to the neighborhood earlier, but I had to work late. Anyway, I'm not here tonight to welcome you. Actually I'm kind of rattled, you know, kinda upset. The side of my house was egged tonight."

"What? Egged? I don't understand. What does 'egged' mean? I've never heard that term before."

"It means hit with eggs. I think your boys did it."

"Did what?"

"Somebody threw raw eggs against the side of my house. It has left a slimy mess."

"I'm shocked. I never heard of such a thing," I said. "Why don't you come in, Barry?" I showed Barry into the kitchen.

By now, Andi had come downstairs, curious as to what was happening.

"What's going on?"

"Andi. This is our neighbor, Barry. He says the side of his house was egged tonight. By our boys."

"Really? But they're asleep. Besides, they wouldn't do something like that. Let me check on them. You know this is our first night in our new house."

"I am really sorry to upset you, but...I know our kids, Rich and Ben, are friends of Drew's. Maybe he can explain."

Andi went upstairs to check the kids. They appeared to be sound asleep.

"I think you're are mistaken, Barry. The boys are asleep and have been asleep now for several hours."

"Please, Andi and Herb, come outside to see the side of my house," Barry said.

We followed Barry outside. His outdoor lights were on, and he had a flashlight. The side of his house, opposite our driveway and immediately across from Drew and Scott's rooms, was done in white siding just like ours. Only his was splattered with egg yolks and shells stuck to the wall. Bits of shell and glistening gook stuck in the grass below as well.

Andi saw this and immediately went back into the house, into the kitchen. Sure enough, a half-dozen eggs were missing from the fridge.

I woke the boys. I whispered so as not to wake Molly. "Wake up, you guys. We know you are awake. And if you're not, you need to be. Greg, Drew, Scott. You have some explaining to do."

The boys wandered sheepishly down from their bedrooms to the kitchen.

"Dad, I swear I didn't do anything. I've been sleeping. Honestly," said Greg. "I'm going back to sleep."

"Greg's telling the truth," Scott said. "He didn't do anything. Drew and I did it."

"We were just having some fun with Rich and Ben," Drew said.

"Some fun, huh? We don't think it's funny at all. I want you and Scott to get dressed. Now. You're going to go next door and clean up your mess. There is a ladder in the garage. You'll also find a bucket there, along with some rags and soap. And you need to apologize to Mr. Aver. Now!" I spoke as sternly as I could, without showing my true feelings. I actually thought it was kind of funny. How in the world did they do it? The two houses weren't that close together. Maybe twenty yards. Did they throw the eggs from inside the house, or did they sneak outside to do their mischief? Questions for another time.

Drew and Scott went upstairs, got dressed, and went next door with the ladder and cleaning supplies. They placed them at the base of the Aver house.

And then they ran.

The Truth. What Is the Truth?

JENNIFER JUMPED UP. THE WINE she was drinking did little to calm the anger she felt upon hearing Tola's confession.

"A *son*? You have a son? And you never told me?" Jennifer was screaming at Tola. Her voice could be heard throughout the apartment complex. The chirping cicadas, a constant background noise, suddenly ceased. It seemed as though whoever was out there was listening. No private conversation going on here.

"What else haven't you told me, Tola? How old is this boy? Do I know his mother? Are you still seeing her? Are you *sleeping* with her? What should I think? Why did you choose to tell me tonight, during our first trip to Cambodia?"

Jennifer was enraged. Her face turned red, and she began to cry. She felt sorry for herself. She felt betrayed. She wanted to hit Tola and came toward him to do so. As she lunged toward him he grabbed her and pulled her close to him. He spoke in a quiet and calm manner as he tried to defuse her emotions.

"Jennifer, please calm down. I am so sorry. I knew this would upset you. Perhaps this is why I didn't tell you before. I guess I was afraid I'd lose you. If you promise to listen, I will try to explain."

Jennifer abruptly pulled away and faced him straight on. "Tola, you have hurt me so badly. Our relationship can never be the same. I will try to listen, but I am in shock." She continued to cry.

They sat down across from one another. Tola began his confession. "I met Alice in a restaurant. She was a waitress and was very nice to my friends and me. I was immediately attracted to her, but I did nothing to pursue her that evening. Turns out she was also a schoolteacher, and she taught at the same school where my niece, Donna, attends. Donna was in a school play, and I was asked to go. I went, and there was Alice. She remembered me, we talked, and I took her home after the play. I made love to her that night, and she became pregnant. This all happened before I met you, Jennifer. I have no regrets, but I am sorry you feel hurt. This happened and it is done. I will come back a better man in my next life. I cannot change anything. Alice moved away before she had the baby. I see them only a few times a year. But they recently moved back to Philadelphia."

Jennifer rose from her chair and began pacing the floor. She didn't know how to respond. She knew Tola was a man from a different culture than hers. That is one of the things that had initially attracted her to him. But his lack of regret, his cavalier attitude toward his fathering a child—these were hard for her to accept.

"Tola. This marriage is over. I want you to leave the apartment. Go and do…whatever you want. But I don't want you here with me. I can't stand to even look at you."

"Jennifer, are you sure you mean this? How will we explain this to our family, our friends? Aren't you acting impulsively? Can't we give it some time?"

"No. I've made up my mind," Jennifer said. "Now get out!"

———◆———

Long Trip Home

Tola packed his things quickly and left the apartment. He took a cab to a nearby hotel. He checked into a room, unpacked his bags, and immediately called Jennifer. After about ten rings, he slammed down the phone in anger. He was enraged. He was perspiring profusely.

"How could she just throw me out? What did I do to deserve her wrath?" He wasn't ready for sleep. It was too early, and besides, he was too upset. He decided to take a walk.

The streets were quiet, save for the occasional tuk-tuk motorbikes zooming past. He was very familiar with the streets of Phnom Penh. He knew it wasn't safe at night to stroll the dark streets. Yet he didn't care. He just kept walking.

Until he came upon a woman. A very pretty woman. Cambodian.

"Want some company, mister? I can give you a very good time. My apartment is just down the next street. Would you like?"

"How much do you charge?" Tola asked.

"How much you got, mister?"

"Come with me to my hotel, and I'll give you fifty dollars, US. You stay with me until I say go. OK?"

"You're a very smart man. You will not be disappointed, mister. My name is Rama."

They walked back to Tola's hotel.

———

Tola told Rama to undress as he watched. She was wearing a black one-piece silk sarong. The garment hid her firm, slender body well. She kicked off her stiletto heels, and then crawled into bed before she removed her bra and underwear. Tola became immediately aroused.

Tola's back was to Rama as he hurriedly began to take off his clothes. He sat on the side of the bed as he removed his shoes and socks and unbuttoned his shirt. His trousers came last. He dropped them to the floor along with the rest of his clothes, and jumped into bed.

Rama awaited him with open arms. Tola mounted her. She was moist and ready for him. He entered her and began. But then something very strange came over him. He felt a pain unlike any he had ever felt. Had he climaxed too soon?

He reached for his groin. It felt very wet. He looked at his hand. It was covered with blood. He went unconscious before he knew the truth. Tola was dead.

Rama felt his stillness. The smell of Tola's ejaculate permeated the room. She pushed him aside and removed her knife from his private parts. She then used the bed sheets to wipe the blood from the knife and replaced it in her bra. Her body was covered with Tola's blood. She cleaned herself as best she could and then she ran to the bathroom.

Rama showered and got dressed. She picked up Tola's wallet from the night table beside the bed. It contained plenty of cash and several credit cards. She took the cash and left the cards. Then she slipped out of the room and went back out into the night.

———

A Natural Reaction

Jennifer rose from a fitful sleep. It was the first time she and Tola had been apart in many months. And it was the first time she had ever demanded they be apart. She was still emotionally hurting from their fight. She could think of nothing else. She was trying not to doubt herself. Had she acted too hastily, too harshly?

The sun was just beginning to rise. It shone through the bamboo shades in her bedroom.

But it was another kind of light that caught her attention. Flashing lights, the kind on police cars and ambulances. A second after she'd noticed the flashing lights, her telephone began to ring, and then there was a loud knocking on her door.

Bang! Bang! Bang!

She jumped up from her bed and pulled on her robe.

"Just a minute!" she called out to whoever was at the door. She picked up the phone.

"Hello."

"Mrs. Saam? Mrs. Jennifer Saam?"

"Speaking. Who is this?"

More knocking. *Bang! Bang!* Flashing lights shone in the window.

"This is Officer Hy of the Phnom Penh Police Department. I am in my car outside your apartment. Could you please open your door? We need to talk."

"What is this about? Why are you here? What time is it?" Jennifer hung up the phone. Was she really awake? Or was she dreaming?

Jennifer staggered to the door and peered through the peephole. A uniformed police officer was standing in the hall. Jennifer began to tremble as she realized she wasn't dreaming. She reluctantly opened the door.

"Sorry to wake you. I am Officer Lou. My partner, Officer Hy, is outside in the car. He is the one who called you."

"I need you to come with me to the police station, Mrs. Saam. Please get dressed, and we will take you there now."

"Can you tell me more? Am I being arrested? Can I make a phone call? Do I need a lawyer? I'm an American citizen, you know. I have rights."

"No, ma'am. I can't tell you more. And I can't answer any of your questions. I really can't. Please get ready. I will wait for you outside."

———————

Jennifer washed her face, combed her hair, and brushed her teeth. She then pulled on a pair of jeans and a T-shirt. She looked out her window. The two police officers were standing by their car, smoking and chatting and laughing. They seemed not to be paying attention to Jennifer or anything else. They were just waiting for her. She thought that odd, but she decided to take advantage of the situation.

Rather than going down immediately, Jennifer decided to call Srey. She dialed the phone and Srey answered on the first ring.

"Srey. This is Jennifer. There are two policemen outside my apartment. They are waiting for me to come out. They want to take me to the police station. I don't know why. They won't tell me anything. I am very scared. What should I do?"

"Jennifer. Why are you calling me? Where is Tola?"

"I don't know. We had a quarrel last night, and he left. I haven't seen him since then."

"Oh...Well, I suggest you go with the police. I will meet you at the station. Try not to worry. I know that is difficult, but try."

———————

Jennifer came out of her apartment. She walked over to the black-and-white police car. Officer Lou helped her get in the back of the car and off they rode to the police station. Officer Hy drove. No sirens, no flashing lights. No one uttered a word. The car reeked of cigarette smoke. The stench made Jennifer choke and cough.

They arrived at the police station. Officer Hy dropped Jennifer and Officer Lou at the entrance. The sign on the station was written in Khmer. If there weren't police cars parked everywhere, she wouldn't have known where she was.

Officer Lou led her to a meeting room. There was a large mirror on the back wall. Jennifer had seen enough crime shows on TV to recognize an interrogation room when she saw one. The mirror looked like a two-way. The walls of the room were painted green. The room was dimly lit by a single exposed light bulb at the end of a wire dangling from the ceiling. The stench of tobacco smoke was as strong in the room as it had been in the car.

Officer Hy joined them and asked Jennifer to seat herself at the square table. Officer Lou sat opposite Jennifer. Hy stood by the door, which was now closed.

Jennifer spoke first. "Why am I here? I demand to know why you brought me here."

"Mrs. Saam, Do you know where your husband is?" asked Officer Lou.

"No. I can't say that I do. Is this about Tola?"

Officer Lou continued. "Weren't you living at your apartment together?"

"Yes, we were. But I asked him to leave last night."

As soon as Jennifer uttered those words, she regretted it. That was none of their business. Or was it?

"Why did you ask him to leave?"

Jennifer stiffened. "That's a personal matter between my husband and me," she said indignantly.

Officer Lou shook his head slowly. "Actually, it isn't a personal matter. You see, we found your husband's body this morning. He was murdered."

Jennifer was shocked, but she did not begin to cry. She didn't know how to respond. She merely turned pale, broke into a cold sweat, and said nothing. She stared into space, stupefied.

———

Srey had been watching the interrogation from behind the two-way mirror. When Officer Lou said, "He was murdered," she had begun to cry. Tola had been a beloved friend. She didn't suspect Jennifer had had anything to do with his death, though. She also knew the PPPD was not going to allow Jennifer freedom until they got some answers from her.

Srey composed herself, left the observation room, and entered the interrogation room. Jennifer stood to greet her, and they embraced warmly.

Srey then introduced herself to the officers.

"I am Srey. Tola was a very dear friend of mine, and Jennifer is my friend too. Please treat her fairly and with respect. The loss of a loved one is a great burden."

"We know who you are, Srey. We will abide by your request. But until our investigation is complete, we must keep Jennifer in custody."

Srey nodded in understanding. She pulled up a chair next to Jennifer. She explained to Jennifer what was happening.

"Do I need a lawyer?" Jennifer asked her.

Srey said, "Yes. I will find one for you. Jennifer. This is going to be very difficult for you, unless you tell the police everything you know. And everything must be truthful. You will not be permitted to leave here until they are satisfied. Do you understand?"

"Yes," Jennifer said. "I understand. I have nothing to hide. I will tell the police all that I know. I will tell them all that I don't know, too. When do I get my lawyer?"

"Not yet," said Srey.

———◆———

The interrogation began in earnest. Jennifer and Srey sat on one side of the table and Officers Lou and Hy sat on the other side. Behind the two-way mirror sat Dr. Kim, a forensic investigator.

Officer Lou began. "Mrs. Saam, let's talk about last night. You told us you were living with your husband. But then you told us you asked him to leave. Is that correct?"

"Yes."

"Why did you ask him to leave?"

"Because we had an argument."

"What was the argument about?"

"Tola told me he needed to tell me something. He said it was difficult for him to tell me but...Tola told me he had fathered a child, a son. This happened before we were married. I was very angry that he had kept this from me. He was very aloof about it. I accused him of betraying my trust and insisted that our marriage was over. I told him to leave. He did not understand, but he did what I asked. He left." Jennifer finally began to cry. Srey handed her a tissue.

"I knew nothing of this child until just now," Srey said. "I am stunned by this news. Tola never told me, and I'm one of his closest friends."

"Mrs. Saam," Officer Lou said. "Then what happened?"

"What do you mean?"

"After you told him to leave, did Tola say where he would go? Did he pack his belongings? What did he do? What did you do?"

"He packed his suitcase with some clothes and left. He just left. I said to get out, and that's what he did."

"And what did you do next?"

"I suppose I just went to bed. I really don't recall."

"Did he take a cab?"

"Yes. At least, I think he did."

"Did you try to follow him?"

"No."

Officer Lou looked Jennifer directly in the eyes. Jennifer met his gaze without blinking.

"Evidently, he took a cab to the Hotel Puncak," Officer Lou said. "That's where we found his body. Have you ever been to the Hotel Puncak?"

"No. Never."

"Do you know where it is?"

"No."

"Did he phone you from the hotel?"

"Not that I am aware of. There was one call last night after he left, but no one was on the line when I picked up."

"Very well. We will stop now. Srey, you may leave. Mrs. Saam, you may not. I am afraid we may have more questions for you tomorrow."

Srey asked if she could talk to Jennifer privately before leaving. The officers consented.

"Jennifer, I will find a lawyer and bring him here tomorrow. Stay safe tonight. I will return in the morning."

Jennifer was led out of the interrogation room. She was photographed and fingerprinted, and taken to a holding cell where she was to spend the night. As she entered the cell, she saw a woman sitting on the side of a bed, weeping.

———◆———

IT'S A SMALL WORLD AFTER ALL

"Why are you crying?" Jennifer asked the young woman. "I suppose that's a stupid question, considering where we are. But I am so very frightened. I could really use someone to talk to. Do you speak English?" Jennifer reached out and offered the woman a tissue. It was the one Srey had handed her during her interrogation. It was still damp from her own tears.

The woman stopped crying and looked up at Jennifer. She accepted the tissue and dried her large blue eyes. "My name is Raylynn Mack. I live in Phnom Penh, although I am originally from Hawaii." She offered Jennifer a smile. Jennifer noticed her freckled face and reddish hair. She also saw how frail and thin Raylynn appeared. Jennifer wondered if she was ill.

"Hello, Raylynn. My name is Jennifer. I live in Phnom Penh, too. I'm originally from Pennsylvania. Nice to meet you." Jennifer offered Raylynn her hand in a gesture of friendship.

"Nice to meet you, too," Raylynn said. She took Jennifer's hand and squeezed it. She did not let go. They embraced.

They simply held one another in silence.

Jennifer began to wonder about Raylynn's situation. She had many questions.

"What can I say to this woman? What should I say? Why is she here?

"Is she an agent of the police, placed here to get me to incriminate myself?

"Is she thinking the same thing about me? What is her story?

"Should I take a chance and share my thoughts with her? Would that be foolish?

"No. I have nothing to hide. I did nothing wrong. Yet, what if the police…I feel so conflicted. It feels so comforting to be held, even by a stranger. And I really want to talk. I need to talk.

"Raylynn seems harmless. But is she? Why is she here? She is so thin, so very frail.

"We certainly are not friends. We just met. We are in jail together, for God's sake.

"Coincidence? Maybe. Maybe not. But I have to take a chance."

Jennifer broke their embrace. She slipped down and sat on the edge of the cot. Raylynn sat next to her.

Raylynn brushed back her hair, which had fallen over her face. She looked Jennifer directly in the eye.

"Raylynn. I came from the United States. I am here in Cambodia to do good work. My husband and I, we are…or rather, we were living in an apartment in Phnom Penh." Jennifer suddenly realized there was no more *we* with Tola. Tola was gone. Dead. The meaning of that suddenly hit her. "How am I ever going to manage without him?" she thought.

She began again. She whispered to Raylynn, fearful that someone might overhear her. She glanced around as she spoke quietly, her fingers covered her lips.

"My plan is to reach out and help the people of Cambodia. I have plans to start a business. I want to create jobs. I want to better the lives of the people here. I want to prepare them for a possible better life. I want to work with the children—"

"Stop!" Raylynn jumped up from the cot. A huge smile came over her face.

"Jennifer. I can't believe this. What a coincidence! I work in a school as a caregiver to Cambodian orphans. The school is called Pursat Orphanage and is located nearly four hours away by automobile."

Jennifer turned away from Raylynn and looked up at the ceiling of the jail. She felt blessed.

Raylynn was crying as she told her story. "I am here because of a misunderstanding. I am so frightened. It's all a mistake, Jennifer. You see, I borrowed a car from a friend to come to Phnom Penh on my day off. Evidently, the car was listed as stolen. The police stopped me and arrested me. I am waiting for my friend to come to the station to get me out of here. Trust me, I am not a car thief. Hopefully, my friend will be able to explain. I was allowed to call him, and he is on his way here."

Jennifer was relieved. She could relax. She had made a new friend.

"I am sure you will be fine soon," Jennifer said. She yawned. "I am very tired. If you will excuse me, I need to take a nap."

Jennifer walked over to the cot, it was hard and smelled of urine. But she was too exhausted to care. She lay down on the cot and fell asleep almost instantly. She had accepted Raylynn's story as truth. It enabled her to rest.

Truth? Jennifer would learn. She was a very trusting person. Reality would soon change that. She wasn't in Philly anymore.

———— ◆ ————

Relief

The screeching, sliding noise of the metal cell door awakened Jennifer. She looked up from where she lay on the mat to see a Cambodian man dressed in a white lab coat. He wore dark-rimmed glasses. Jennifer thought he looked intelligent. He had an air of calm about him that set her at ease.

She struggled to her feet. She felt achy and uncomfortable. The cold, hard cot had taken its toll on her muscles. She raised her arms and exhaled loudly as she attempted to stretch.

"Who are you?" Jennifer said.

"I am Dr. Kim. Don't be afraid. It is my job to determine how your husband died. I would like you to leave this cell with me now to view his body. Are you willing to come with me?"

"Do I have a choice?" asked Jennifer.

Dr. Kim ignored the question. "Please follow me."

He held Jennifer's arm and led her out of the cell.

Before they left, Jennifer looked around for Raylynn. She was gone.

"Oh no, when did she go? Was I asleep so soundly that I didn't hear her leave?" Jennifer thought.

"Where is Raylynn?" Jennifer asked Dr. Kim.

"She was released earlier."

"Oh. I suppose her friend came and got her freed?" asked Jennifer.

"I am sorry, but I don't know. She was not my case."

Dr. Kim guided Jennifer down a long, dimly lit hallway. They passed a number of doors, all clearly marked by Khmer writing. None of the signs meant anything to Jennifer. Finally, they came to their destination.

Dr. Kim unlocked the entrance door to the laboratory. This room sheltered all of the deceased victims in the homicide system. The room seemed very sterile, like an operating room. Massive stainless steel doors lined the perimeter of the lab. Shiny examining tables and exotic-looking light fixtures, mirrors, and cameras hung down from the ceiling. Computer consoles were placed opposite each table.

Jennifer looked anxiously around the room for Tola. All she saw was the equipment. She was strangely disappointed. Nervous, she tried to be humorous.

"This isn't going to be like a viewing at a funeral, I imagine," she said to Dr. Kim.

She was scared. It was very cold in the laboratory, yet she was sweating profusely. Dr. Kim gave Jennifer a facemask.

"Here, put this on. It will help you deal with the odors."

Jennifer complied.

Dr. Kim opened one of the steel doors. A large black plastic bag lay inside one of the drawers. He pulled the drawer out. Wheels dropped down to the floor, and he rolled the drawer toward Jennifer.

"Are you ready? Please take a deep breath and try to be calm. This will not be easy. It never is," said Dr. Kim.

Dr. Kim pulled the bag open and revealed Tola's head and shoulders. Jennifer stared at Tola's face and began to weep. Smelling the stench of death and seeing him in the flesh ended all denial for her.

Dr. Kim rolled a chair for Jennifer to sit on before she could fall to the floor.

"He was a victim of homicide," Dr. Kim said. "He bled to death. This is why his skin appears gray and sallow. We found him many hours after he died."

"How did he die?" Jennifer asked, still sobbing. Her words were muffled by the mask.

"He was killed with a knife."

"Do you know who did this?"

"Not yet," said Dr. Kim, and paused for a moment. "But we know it was not you."

Jennifer was speechless. They knew she was innocent!

"When you are ready, you may leave here," said Dr. Kim. "Srey is waiting for you outside to take you home."

The Beginnings of a Foundation

———◆———

JENNIFER WALKED OUT OF THE police station. Srey was waiting for her. "Jennifer. How are you feeling?"

They embraced as Jennifer cried.

"Oh, Srey. I am free, yet I feel so unclean. The jail cell was disgusting. I feel so sad. Tola is dead, and I am now all alone in a country I hardly know. I feel frightened. Who killed Tola? Why was he killed? Please, Srey. Let's get away from here as quickly as possible. I never want to see this place again. Ever."

Srey held Jennifer's arm as she led her away from the station.

"I understand, Jennifer. Lots of questions and very few answers. In so many ways, this is not a good place for a woman to be. Come with me," Srey said. "I'm parked around the back."

Jennifer asked, "Can you take me home? To my apartment? I need to shower and eat something."

Srey drove Jennifer home and dropped her off at the entry gate to her apartment complex. An armed, uniformed guard greeted her and allowed her to pass into the barbed-wire-fenced courtyard.

Jennifer lived in an international compound, occupied by persons from all over the world. Security was important to the residents living here. Everyone was vulnerable to personal assault at any time. Cambodia was a very dangerous place for foreigners.

As Jennifer exited the car, Srey said, "I have given a great deal of thought about the ideas you proposed earlier. We should talk soon."

"I would like that, Srey. Please call me after dinner."

———◆———

The phone rang at seven o'clock that evening. It was Srey.

"Are you available to meet this evening?" she asked Jennifer.

Jennifer was eager to see Srey. "I am really tired, but I guess I can spend a few hours. Why don't you come over to my apartment? I'll brew some tea."

———◆———

Srey arrived at Jennifer's apartment less than twenty minutes later. She was wearing a dark purple dress with matching amethyst earrings. Her black hair was pulled back into a braid. Her white sneakers looked out of place until you realized that Jennifer's apartment complex was undergoing major construction. Mud was everywhere.

Jennifer greeted Srey dressed in blue jeans and a yellow T-shirt. Her wet blond hair was brushed back off of her face. "Please come in, Srey. The tea is almost ready. Why don't we sit outside on the patio overlooking the courtyard?"

Jennifer led Srey to the patio, which was located behind the master bedroom. They sat down opposite one another on bamboo rockers. Srey spoke first. "Jennifer. I am so sorry for your loss. I only hope that the unexpected death of your husband has made you even more determined to settle here in Cambodia and do good work."

"Thank you, Srey. Even without Tola, I believe more than ever that I am destined to stay and work here. The stunning landscapes, historic temples and the beauty of its people often mask its wrenching poverty and its horrific recent history. But I hope to unmask the poverty and help to teach the Cambodian people to use their strengths to rebuild their society. I am only one woman. But I have a great deal of passion and energy. Especially when it comes to Cambodia."

"Very well then," Srey said. "Let me share with you a cautionary tale. You must hear this from me, your friend. It will be painful to your heart, but the lessons learned may guide you along a better path."

"What are you talking about?" asked Jennifer. Srey had never seemed so serious before.

"Please listen. Cambodia is a nation ripe for exploitation. Decades of war and the nearly two million who were killed left it one of the poorest nations on earth. Because of its lack of resources, along with a lack of an educated middle class, family planning, sufficient food, and adequate shelter, the Cambodian people have succumbed to graft and corruption.

"Stories of people selling children, whether for prostitution, slave labor, or adoption, are common and all too real. No one knows how many of those children were true orphans or merely babies of Cambodian mothers who had been tricked into selling them. Don't you agree that an adoptive parent has the right to expect that the child they are adopting is truly orphaned or abandoned?"

"Of course," Jennifer said. "It is simple human decency. A matter of basic trust."

"Cambodia is a very complicated place. It will not be easy for you. But the potential good you can do far outweighs the risks. I want to work with you as we travel together to make Cambodia a better place. Are you willing to come along?"

Pursat Infant Center

———•———

IN 1998, MOLLY GRADUATED COLLEGE with a degree in elementary education. She was nineteen years old. Before assuming her new teaching job in the United States, she decided to visit her mother in Cambodia. She traveled from John F. Kennedy Airport to Bangkok, Thailand, and then moved on to Cambodia. Riding in a two-engine propeller bombardier that was carrying thirty passengers was not Molly's idea of fun. The flight was noisy and bumpy. But she arrived safely, and that was all that mattered. She exited the airplane in the big city of Phnom Penh. What a relief!

She cleared customs and retrieved her luggage without any trouble. The people she met at the airport were very pleasant and friendly. Before she arrived, she had visions of all kinds of difficulties arising with customs officers and lost luggage. But, as with most things in life, the anxiety and fear was far worse than the reality. She found her way by simply following the signs—even though they were written in Khmer, international symbols and arrows pointed the way.

Then she walked outside to passenger pickup.

It was a clear, sunny day. Not a cloud anywhere. But it was ninety-five degrees and very humid. She began to sweat profusely.

Molly looked for Jennifer. She saw many people of different nationalities scurrying around, walking to and fro. The hustle and bustle seemed no different from what she had seen at the New York and Thailand airports. But no Jennifer. Par for the course. Jennifer was never on time. Ever.

After about thirty minutes, a white Mercedes van pulled up to the curb, and Jennifer poked her head out of the back sliding door. She waved to Molly.

Jennifer got out of the van, gave Molly a jasmine flower necklace, sort of a Cambodian lei, and hugged her. "Welcome to Cambodia, Molly," she said. Molly kissed her mother on the cheek.

"Hi, Mom. Thanks for the flowers. They smell wonderful! You look well. How's it going?"

As she expected, Molly found Jennifer's tone and manner to be distant, not warm as she'd have liked. "Well, I just love it here, Molly," Jennifer said. "Wouldn't want to be anywhere else."

Molly just smiled. It was what she always got from Jennifer. Not much warmth. Not much communication. Molly had stopped trying to understand her mother years ago. Her mother was who she was. She wasn't ever going to change.

"How was your flight? You flew from JFK on Thai Airways, right?" Jennifer knew that. She had suggested the itinerary.

"It was very tiring. As you know, we left at eleven o'clock at night. As soon as I fell asleep, they woke me for a snack. After another couple of hours, I got another wake up. The hostesses were very nice and very pretty. But too attentive for me."

"Oh, Molly. Sorry. Anyway, would you like to see some of Phnom Penh before we go to my apartment? This is my driver. His name is Pot, but we call him Mr. Lucky."

Pot/Mr. Lucky looked like a character from a James Bond movie. Round face, dark and serious eyes. White shirt. Black jacket and pants. Black—even in this heat! He did not speak to Molly. He merely nodded.

"I'm a little tired," Molly said. "But sure, why not. Show me Cambodia!" They left the airport and rode by the Royal Palace. Jennifer described the sights as they passed by.

"This is the residence of the King. Much of Cambodia's wealth is held by the royal family."

"Do they help the poor people? What's the government like?"

"I'm not really sure. But I think it's a lot like the French. The French were here for many years before and during the war. Some parts are like the English. You know. Prime Minister, Monarch, House of Commons. The poor are not treated fairly, but the government is trying to change that. For instance, they are spending a lot on schools."

"Well, that's good."

"There is the Buddhist Temple. Ninety-eight percent of the Cambodian people are Buddhist. And here we are now passing the American Embassy. Armed Cambodian soldiers guard it. No one may go near this embassy without permission."

"Why Cambodian soldiers?"

"I don't know. Perhaps because the embassy is located on Cambodian land?"

"Next is the International Press Club. During the war, correspondents stayed here for food and lodging. It is now a hotel and a restaurant. They have a really neat camera collection. Maybe we'll have lunch here one afternoon."

"That would be nice," Molly said.

"Pot, please drive downtown along the river."

Mr. Lucky turned the van toward the river. The previously smooth paved streets suddenly turned uneven, rocky, and bumpy.

All of a sudden a myriad of small motorcycles buzzed by their van. Each tuk-tuk bike carried a driver and several passengers, or lots of cargo, usually vegetables, fruit, or fish.

The tuk-tuks and their cargo gave the city air a unique smell. Not unpleasant, but sort of a combination of sweet fish and bananas. Molly's jasmine necklace complemented the odors. But Molly was more interested in seeing the orphanage and the people Jennifer worked with.

"Can we visit the orphanage? I'd love to see the children and meet the nannies," Molly said.

"Certainly. We can do that tomorrow," Jennifer replied. "It is about a four-hour drive from here. Why don't we head to the apartment now, Mr. Lucky."

———

Pot turned the van away from the river road, onto smoother paving. About five minutes later, they pulled up to an armed compound. There was a ten-foot-high cement wall topped with barbed wire surrounding the property, and a brightly colored red-and-gold ornate gate stood at the entrance. A guard dressed in denim blue jeans and a shirt emblazoned with a gold star-shaped badge greeted them. He wore a blue baseball cap bearing the same badge. The guard immediately recognized Mr. Lucky and opened the gate. He welcomed them all with a salute and a smile.

They drove into the compound.

"This is where I live," Jennifer explained to Molly. "It's an international apartment complex. Approximately one hundred foreigners stay here. Mostly business people, but we have teachers, doctors, diplomats, and building engineers. I believe that everyone who lives here works to help better the Cambodian nation. I hope I am right about that. You know my friend Srey? That's what she says. She ought to know. After all, she is the owner of this place. And she knows nearly everyone in Phnom Penh.

"I pay my rent to her. She is very kind and helpful. We work together on the Foundation and the Pursat Children's Center."

Molly followed Jennifer up a flight of brick-red ceramic tile steps to the apartment. The door was made of dark mahogany and was trimmed with polished brass carvings. Jennifer opened the door with her key and Molly entered.

Mr. Lucky followed them in with Molly's luggage. He placed them in what was to be Molly's bedroom and said, "OK. See you tomorrow morning. I drive to Pursat, yes?"

"Yes. Please be here at six o'clock. Thank you, Pot," said Jennifer.

"OK. I see you," said Pot.

———

"This place is lovely, Mom."

"Thanks, Molly. I find it very comfortable. You don't find too many two-bedroom apartments with air conditioning and a swimming pool!" Jennifer smiled. "Thanks to Srey, my rent is affordable. With my savings, I've managed to furnish the place with things found all over the countryside. I've met the people who have made every piece of furniture in this place, except the beds and mattresses."

Molly laughed. "That's amazing."

"When we go to Pursat tomorrow, I'll take you to the factory where they carve stone into artistic masterpieces."

"I look forward to seeing it."

———

Molly unpacked her luggage while Jennifer prepared a dinner of fresh vegetables, rice, and some local fish all mixed together in a wok with a flavorful fish sauce, oil, and white Cambodian wine. The pungent aroma of the cooking spread throughout the entire apartment.

Both Jennifer and Molly used chopsticks. Dinner was delicious.

After dinner they went down to the pool, where they lay on lounges and enjoyed the quiet bubbling of the water. The heat of the day gave way to a mild, less oppressive evening. But it was still hot. Molly closed her eyes and fell asleep.

———

"Molly, time to get up. Mr. Lucky will be here in an hour."

Molly had slept her first night in Cambodia in a lounge chair by the pool. How funny was that! She awakened upon Jennifer's calling, stretched, and had a good chuckle. Then she ran up the stairs into the apartment to shower and get ready for the day.

———

Mr. Lucky arrived promptly at six am. He greeted Jennifer and Molly with the Khmer words for hello: "Seusaday."

"Seusaday, Pot," Jennifer replied.

Pot closed the van's sliding door after Jennifer and Molly had gotten in. The passenger seat was already filled with packages. Jennifer explained that they were supplies for the orphanage.

"Pot, we did not have breakfast yet. Please stop at the French bakery, OK?"

"OK."

Ten minutes later they arrived at the bakery.

———————

A Postcard from Molly

Dear Dad:

You can't help but to fall in love with Cambodia. The physical land-scape, the wildlife, elephants, monkeys, the trees, the flowers, the climate. The smell of the air. Like being on a tropical island. And yet Cambodia is a third world country. Its people have been decimated by poverty, by war, by genocide. Yet they are so docile, so friendly, so happy in their lives.

Mom couldn't have picked a more difficult challenge for her life's work.

I'm fine. See you soon.

Love, Molly

———————

Trip to Pursat

The bakery was located in a dark-brown wooden building that looked like a rustic barn. The entire front was open to the street, and inside were tables with white linen tablecloths and chairs neatly arranged along a lattice fence. At the back of the building were two large glass display counters holding a vast assortment of pastries. Chocolate éclairs, fruit cobblers, crullers, beignets, croissants. The variety and the colorful presentation were most impressive. The fragrances of the pastries and the fresh-ground coffees were prevalent throughout. Just entering the establishment was a treat to the senses.

The proprietor, a Cambodian woman named Cha, was dressed in a white apron. She wore a chef's hat that dwarfed her tiny but pleasant face. Cha appeared from behind the counter to greet Jennifer and Molly. (Mr. Lucky remained in the van.) She was so short, she could barely see over the counter.

"Hello, Cha," Jennifer said. "How are you today? I'd like you to meet my daughter, Molly. Molly, say hello to Cha. We're on our way to Pursat. I thought we'd stop on the way and enjoy your fine bakery."

"*Bonne matin, mes amies.* How nice to see you, Jennifer. Can I offer you some of my pastries? Just came out of the oven. Very fresh."

Jennifer recommended the croissants and Danish to Molly. "The coffee is very strong here, not at all like you're used to in America," Jennifer said. "I strongly advise you not to try it."

Despite Jennifer's caution, Molly ordered the Danish and a cup of coffee. "I like strong coffee. The stronger the better," she said.

"OK," Jennifer said. "I guess you can decide for yourself. Anyway, I think I'll have a coffee and a fruit cobbler please." Molly smiled at Jennifer.

Cha gave Molly her Danish and Jennifer her cobbler. "I will bring the coffee to your table. Please be seated."

The coffee was served in a French press. Cha pressed it at their table, and then poured the coffee into two white porcelain cups.

She left the press for refills. Molly inhaled the aroma and took a sip. Jennifer was right. It was very strong and very hot. "Wow! You weren't kidding. This is the strongest, hottest coffee I've ever had! But it is delicious. I love the flavor and the body." The pastries were also first-rate. They both oohed and aahed as they enjoyed them.

Jennifer paid the bill. Cha thanked them for coming and also expressed her gratitude to Jennifer for bringing Molly.

Before they left, they both used the restroom. "You'll need to squat over a porcelain-covered hole. No plumbing this far out of the city," Jennifer told Molly.

Back at the van, Jennifer gave Mr. Lucky his instructions. "On to Pursat. Please stay in the middle of the road. We don't want to find any land mines."

"You're kidding. Aren't you?" Molly asked.

"Not really. There are still lots of unexploded land mines all over Cambodia. But don't worry. Our van has a very strong undercarriage. If we hit a mine, we will survive. At least, I hope so." Jennifer was serious.

Molly didn't know what to think. She suddenly wondered why she felt shaky. Was it the coffee she'd just consumed, or was it her mother's strange view on survival? Or was it just the bumps in the road?

———•———

The road on the way to Pursat was mostly unpaved. It was the dry season, so puddles and ditches were few and far between. But the ride was not at all smooth. After about half an hour of just gazing at the unremarkable countryside, with occasional small farms scattered between the vast emptiness of a scarred landscape, Jennifer broke the silence of the ride.

"Molly. I'd like to share with you a letter I received from a man named Hay Loeuth. He is a victim of a land mine. If you like, I can read it to you. It will help pass the time as we ride toward Pursat. But I caution you, the letter is very sad."

"Please, read it. I'd like to hear it."

"All right. I'll begin.

Kind Lady:

I want to tell you about the suffering that has struck my heart and that I cannot rid myself of. I want to tell you how I feel.

When my legs were blown off by a land mine, I was grief stricken. While those around me were cheerful and happy, I was miserable. I had no strength to struggle and continue in this world. My heart was either full of sorrow or hopelessness.

Living for what? Just a little food to fill the hungry stomach and waiting for the end of the day.

I lost all my sense of being and self-esteem. I filled myself instead with cowardice, fear, and despair. I did not want to live. The words wouldn't stop ringing in my ears: 'I am an amputee.' There is no reason for living found in these words.

Always under stress from the disregard of other people.

Living like a turtle that hides its face into its shell when it meets animals or men. Like a bird that gets its food from the female. Or like the kind of tree that grows on another tree. I am a parasite.

Everything that I could do before—walk, stand, sit, jump, run—I can do no more.

If I had money and went to the store to buy something to eat, the owner yelled at me to go away. How humiliated I was. He did not welcome me as a customer, but as a beggar. I had money to pay, but he took me for a beggar.

The heart of the amputee is filled with nothing but sorrow and shame.

That is the gift of land mines to the amputee.

I try to will my legs to grow back. I have learned that a crab can grow its legs back. Also the earthworm can still survive if parts of its body are broken off.

But what happens to the legs? When will they grow back?

So while waiting to grow back my legs, my stomach feels hungry. It shouts for food.

So I will beg, which is full of shame.

Mud cakes me and flies swarm around me.

But I raise my hands together in respect to ask for charity.

Signed Hay Loeuth.

That's it. Pretty powerful, don't you agree?" asked Jennifer.

Molly was crying. "Do you know this man?"

"Yes, I did. But he died a short time ago. He was a very special young man."

For Once, a "Happy" Story (Everything Is Relative)

MOLLY WAS STILL TEARY-EYED AS a result of the letter her mother Jennifer had just read to her. She couldn't get over the horror of a man losing his limbs out of her mind. And his passionate plea for help.

"What other interesting thoughts do you have, mother? I hope you can relate stories with more cheerful ideas than exploding land mines while we're riding to Pursat."

"As a matter of fact, I can," Jennifer said. She reached over and patted Molly's hand.

"Molly, did Dany Song ever tell you about her life in Cambodia before she escaped to Thailand?"

"No, she never really wanted to share that part of her life," Molly replied. "She talked of the refugee camp, but never much about her life before that."

"Well then, listen to this," said Jennifer. "You know Dany's real name is Siv. Unlike most youngsters, she was fortunate to get a good education during her formative years, something rare for a woman in Cambodia. But she was very smart, and she was able to learn to speak and write English and French in school.

"She earned a living by teaching in an international school in Phnom Penh. Although they were very poor, she provided for her younger brother and her mother. Her father had left the family shortly after her brother was born, when she was still very young. They lived in a wooden hut and subsisted on rice and fruit.

"In the latter part of 1967, when Siv was only eighteen years old, change came to Cambodia. An armed military group called the Khmer Rouge invaded Phnom Penh. Thousands of people were rounded up, taken from their homes by force, and transferred to work camps. Siv Heang Troeng and her family were included.

"They were transported in trucks to a fenced compound outside of Phnom Penh called Kampong. The compound was created from a farm village. The army had transformed the village school buildings into ghettos where the women were to stay. The army also erected temporary shelters for the men and boys.

"The military personnel, all armed and dressed in green uniforms with red armbands, were primarily male. They tended to be very young and meanspirited. They had been trained to despise their captives, even though they were all Cambodian citizens. Their leaders told them that Cambodia was to be transformed into an agricultural state called Angkar. All the educated people were to be turned into workers. The soldiers were strict and short-tempered. Those captives who were not compliant were taken away and killed.

"Every evening, the workers were required to attend a meeting with the soldiers, where the necessity of working hard for the good of Angkar and the village was stressed. Each night, the quantity of the work produced was tallied and disclosed to the workers. Ever increasing standards were set, and everyone was urged to work harder the next day. If they did not perform, they would be killed. Siv and her family tried the best they could.

"They were awoken at dawn, given a meager subsistence breakfast of rice, and transported to the fields.

"At noon, the workers were given an hour for lunch. They would gather on the bank of the river to eat. Most of the workers would eat quickly and try to rest before going back to work.

"One afternoon, Siv lay down on a crude bench. A friend saw her resting there and came to sit beside her. But the bench was fashioned from a pair of unsecured planks, and when her friend sat down the planks buckled together. Siv fell off the bench and cut her bare foot, tearing the underside of her big toe. She began bleeding profusely.

"A young woman soldier saw the accident and came over to cleanse the wound. She wrapped Siv's foot with a cloth bandage. Then she commanded Siv return to work in the wet, muddy, filthy rice paddies.

"Siv had no shoes. She was in a great deal of pain, but she managed to reach the field limping all the way. She worked the rest of the day and nursed her wound as best she could.

"After two weeks, the wound had not healed. Every day Siv finished lunch early to try to make it back to the field at the same time as her fellow workers. But in the morning, there was no way to keep up. Everyone left in a single group as soon as it became light, and she always was the last one to the field.

"One evening, during a community meeting with the workers and the soldiers, Siv sat in the middle of a long line of exhausted women, fighting off the urge to sleep. The soldier began the meeting by calling out a young woman who had stolen a skirt. The soldier's anger was obvious as he stared straight into the woman's face and gestured out to the rice fields. He said, 'Maybe you want to sleep out there.'

"A hush fell over the listeners—two hundred people, or more, suddenly dead silent. Everyone knew what his question really meant.

"The soldier then turned to another young man. The man had jokingly referred to the homemade medicine used by the Khmer Rouge as 'rabbit shit.'

"'You look down on our medicine?' the soldier asked the man. 'Maybe you look down on me, too? I have a place for you.' He pointed out toward the shallow canals that cut through the fields. 'It's easy for me. I don't even have to dig a new hole.'

"The soldier paused briefly, letting his words sink in before he continued. Then he called out one more name.

"'Siv!'

"Siv did not just hear her name; she felt it. Like the hard impact of a shovel to the back of her head. A chill tore her heart away and left her hollow inside. From a few rows away, Siv could see her brother turn toward her in horror. His eyes seemed to be asking her, 'What did you do?'

"The soldier walked over to Siv and stared into her eyes. 'Siv. I watch you every day.' Then he paused.

"'You are a hard worker. Even though you are hurt, you still go to work every day. And you never complain.'

"Siv felt her heart begin to beat again as relief washed over her. The soldier continued. Turning away from Siv, he faced the rest of the group. 'You all must learn to follow the example set by such a hard worker. Forget your own problems, and concentrate on the work demanded of you.'"

———◆———

"Well, that's the story. Can you imagine surviving that kind of pressure and intimidation?"

"No," Molly replied. "I can't. I've always respected Dany. I knew her life here was difficult. But this is truly remarkable. What a story!"

Jennifer just smiled.

Pursat Orphanage

MR. LUCKY BEEPED HIS HORN as he turned the white Mercedes van onto a sandy pathway. Suddenly, ten little boys and girls ran out from a white cinder-block building through clouds of dust to greet the van. They were all cheering and shouting, smiling and laughing as though they had not a care in the world.

The children of school age, five and older, were dressed in white shirts and blue trousers. They all wore Nike sneakers with white socks. The younger children were dressed in brightly colored T-shirts and shorts. None of the children looked malnourished or sick in any way. They were well-groomed and happy kids.

As soon as the van stopped, Molly jumped out. At Jennifer's urging, Molly had worn a white oxford button-down shirt and a pair of blue Dockers. She looked just like the children!

Now the children were upon her, jumping and cheering with their arms outstretched to hug her. The welcome was overwhelming and brought tears to Molly's eyes. Molly simply stood still, taking in the affection.

Jennifer watched with joy. She had experienced similar moments many times before. It was these moments that sustained her at difficult times in her work. Now she hoped Molly, her daughter, might feel the same and want to join her in helping the children of Pursat.

Jennifer called to the three nannies who were standing in the background while the children clustered around Molly. "Ngen, Mom, and Hour, please take the children so we might have a quieter visit."

Putting her arm around Molly, Jennifer proudly introduced her to the nannies and the now-quieted youngsters. "This is my daughter, Molly."

"Pleased to meet you, Molly," they said in unison.

"Happy to meet you, too," Molly replied.

———◆———

THEARY

Theary was four years old. She was the kind of child who stood out from the crowd. First and foremost, her eyes were striking. They were bright and shiny, a sort of grayish-brown color. A radiant glow emanated from her smile. Her hair had natural highlights of pale brown with blond streaks. Her flawless skin was caramel.

She had lived in the orphanage since she was an infant. She had always been a sickly, lethargic child who never seemed to gain much weight. She was prone to viruses and minor infections. She would fatigue easily and become short of breath.

After many examinations and tests, it was discovered that Theary suffered from a condition called Ventricular Septal Defect or VSD.

Theary had a hole in the lower chamber of her heart. The only way she would have a chance at a long, healthy life would be to have an operation to patch the hole.

Theary underwent surgery at the Phnom Penh Heart Center, where the tiny hole was patched with Gore-Tex, a synthetic waterproof fabric permeable to air and water that is used for vascular grafts. Dr. Sokchan, the doctor who cares for the children in Pursat, was in attendance during the operation.

Theary was discharged from the hospital after a week, whereupon she stayed at the home of her nanny's relative in Phnom Penh. She stayed there for a month, recuperating. A large scar runs from just below her neck to where her rib cage ends, but she is now gaining weight and is as happy as can be.

Theary was just one of the children in the Pursat orphanage who have moderate to serious medical problems. STDs like HIV, AIDS, and syphilis are not uncommon in Pursat. Sick children require more care and therefore incur more expenses than healthy children. In addition to the costs of medicine and procedures, each time a child is treated, they need to be transported to Phnom Penh, because the medical care in Pursat is insufficient.

Jennifer's foundation was always appealing for funds—for medical treatments, extraordinary transportation costs, or special projects to help the children. Usually, the parents and families of the adopted children in America provided the necessary money. When a deficit arose, Jennifer gave what she could from her own savings. Sometimes, even the Cambodian government helped out. But not very often.

Molly's Choice

———————

Just as Jennifer had hoped, Molly fell in love with the children at Pursat Orphanage. How could she not? They were warm and deserving of her love.

Molly willingly jumped in with both feet. She viewed the orphanage as a worthwhile challenge. She was certain that her knowledge and experience as an elementary school teacher would enable her to give the children there tools that would greatly benefit them in their lives.

"Mother, if it's OK with you, I would like to spend my summer in Cambodia here with you. I could work as a volunteer and assist you in your foundation activities. What do you think?"

Jennifer didn't hesitate for a second.

"I would be thrilled to have you, Molly. Of course, you'll have to extend your visa to be able to stay here longer, but I'm sure that won't be a problem," said Jennifer.

"Also, I'll have to call Marc and tell him. And Dad. Though I think Marc might want to come here and volunteer, too." Molly liked that idea. After all, Marc was soon to become her husband.

"I think that would be great," said Jennifer.

———————

And so it was. Molly stayed on for the summer, and Marc traveled to Cambodia to join her. Little did I know that their summer vacation would challenge and change our family forever.

Molly's first assignment was to oversee the renovations of the building at Pursat Orphanage.

There were drawings to follow. The drawings called for the newly restored building to house the infant program. The building was designed to house up to twenty children and their caregivers. The building as it was could house only ten.

The building was to consist of two large rooms, each roughly nine by twelve feet, to be used as nurseries and sleeping areas. These living areas were to be connected by a small room set up as a play area. The entire interior was to be painted, and tile was to be laid on the floor and halfway up the walls to make cleaning the facility easier. Each living area was to have new electrical wiring and new ceiling fans. Electrical outlets would be placed out of reach of little hands.

Each nanny was to be given a new wooden bed, along with a locking wooden bedside table for storing personal possessions.

The drawings called for a porch, where the children and nannies would spend much of their time and eat their meals. The porch area was to be enclosed with a banister, so that younger children would not fall off the small ledge. Two new bathrooms, accessible through each of the living areas, were to be constructed from brick and cement. A kitchen was to be built on the end of the building and would be accessible only from the outside.

The entire project was expected to take fourteen days. Under Molly's supervision, it was completed in ten!

———•———

Jennifer and Molly, together with the children and the nannies, planted mango and papaya trees, as well as flower gardens in the front of the porch. Mosquito screening was installed on all of the windows and ventilation slats.

Finally, a play area was located and the land graded in the front of the building. A playground set, constructed of aluminum and coated with vivid yellow, red, and blue paint, was built on the land. It consisted of a slide, all kinds of swings, and many climbing ladders.

After all this was done, at the nannies' request, a Buddhist water blessing was held to celebrate the completion of the renovations. The blessing took about an hour. Monks chanted harmoniously as they wished good luck, safe travel through life, and a long life to all. The blessing was accompanied by a slight sprinkling of holy water. At the end of the ceremony, each participant was given a special wrist tie signifying the blessing just performed.

———•———

Becoming Rath

———

"I believe for every drop of rain that falls, a flower grows."

—Drake, Graham, Shirl, and Stillman

Nasee

A beautiful woman of seventeen, Nasee was married to Chin in a Buddhist Temple. Most couples in their community had been matched by their parents, but Nasee's and Chin's marriage was not arranged. Both sets of parents were deceased.

Nasee was fortunate to know and to love Chin her entire life. They grew up in the same village, went to the same school, and worshiped at the same temple. Their traditional marital blessing came without hesitation. Everyone knew of their love.

So did their babies. Nasee gave birth to four healthy children in less than five years.

Chin was a rice farmer, and the young family was hardly able to make ends meet. They lived in a one-room masonry structure elevated on wooden stilts. It was located near the rice paddy where

Chin worked. Their lives were difficult, and they subsisted on rice and fruits.

Just after the birth of baby number four, a girl named Mona, Nasee contracted malaria. Her fever was very high, and she became too weak to do anything but sweat and sleep.

The family was in crisis. What should they do? Nasee was too ill to nurse the baby. Whatever money they had was now to go for medicine and baby formula. The doctor assured Nasee that she would recover, but it could take several months. And she might never be totally rid of the illness.

Chin summoned Nasee's youngest sister, Donna, to come and help care for Nasee and all the children. She was very capable, but she couldn't stay too long. She had to get back to work on her parents' farm.

"I think we need to seek help and advice from Monk Punna," Chin suggested.

"Why?" asked Nasee, barely conscious. "Do you think he will know what we must do? Can he help us? Will prayers be enough?"

"I don't know if he will have an answer," Chin replied. "But I believe he will offer his thoughts and pray for us."

———

Chin went to the temple to seek an audience with Monk Punna.

Punna had just returned from a visit to his followers in the village. Each day, he tended to the prayers of the sick, the troubled, and the needy. Chin found him in the temple burning incense and meditating before a statue of Buddha. Punna was dressed in his orange robes.

Chin waited until Punna was finished meditating. When Chin was summoned to meet with the monk, he told Punna about Nasee's illness and explained to him that their family was in despair.

"I need your advice. Nasee and I need your prayers and your help."

Punna thought. He chanted a prayer, and then he responded, all the while holding his hands out to Chin.

"You will choose understanding. You must not be sad. Buddha says, 'Life is never ending. Each of our souls ebbs and flows from one time to another. Your despair shall pass.'

"Chin, if you and Nasee can find it in your hearts, bring the baby Mona to the Temple, and I will show her a new path. Mona will ultimately gain sustenance, and you and Nasee will gain peace. Nasee needs strength to recover. This act of charity will give Nasee and the rest of your family that which they need. Now go and bring me Mona."

Chin bowed to Punna with awe and gratitude. He then hurried back home to Nasee, Donna, and the children.

Chin was puzzled. He thought he understood what Punna was suggesting, but he wasn't sure. Was Punna going to bless the baby and request a charitable act from Chin? And what would that act be? Saying a prayer? Lighting candles? Burning incense? And how would that act, whatever it was, give his family what they needed?

They needed time to rest. They needed time to heal. In short, they needed a simpler life.

Word for word, he related Punna's advice to Nasee.

"Are you certain that is what he said?" asked Nasee.

"Yes, I am sure."

Nasee knew exactly what Punna meant. No doubt, Punna wanted to make her family smaller.

With all the remaining strength she had in her feverish body, she screamed, "No! Not my baby! Not Mona!"

But Chin believed Punna was right. And so, after Nasee had cried herself to sleep, he took baby Mona and wrapped her in a soft white cotton towel. She was none the wiser about what was about to happen. It would change her life forever.

Chin carried Mona to the Buddhist temple and brought her to Punna.

BITTERSWEET IT IS

"Chin," said Punna, "you have made a wise choice. Buddha will bless this child, and your family will gain a newfound energy from your sacrifice."

Punna took Mona and bade Chin good-bye.

With much sadness in his heart, Chin returned to Nasee and watched as she slept. The sun was setting, and the night was upon them.

Nasee would not live to see another sunrise.

———————

Punna placed Mona in a straw basket and delivered her to Pursat Orphanage. The nannies welcomed her and took her from Punna. They placed her in a crib as Punna chanted softly. Then everyone retired to recharge for the coming morning.

Jennifer and Molly returned to Pursat early at dawn after sleeping soundly in a nearby inn. The morning air was hot, humid, and misty. Frogs were croaking, and birds were chirping. The sound of children was everywhere. In particular, there was the sound of a baby crying.

"Come see the new baby!" the children shouted.

Molly was beaming with excitement as soon as she heard the news. She ran into the nursery to see Mona. She had so many questions to ask the nannies.

"What time did the baby arrive? Where did she come from? Is she healthy? She has almost no hair. Is that normal? What happens next? Can I hold her? Can I feed her? Oh my goodness. I am overjoyed that this is happening!"

Jennifer calmly explained to Molly what was about to happen. She had seen it so many times. And each time, it was so bittersweet. It was her choice to be involved with these young lives. But each time, it was so difficult.

"The nannies have already taken the baby's picture. They have posted it on the village bulletin board, together with an official government form describing the child, the date and time of her arrival at the orphanage, and her estimated birth date. Then the clock begins to tick. Ninety days must pass before the baby is legally declared an orphan according to Cambodian law.

"Important questions and answers are not discussed—questions such as, does she have a mother? A father? Is she an orphan according to the American legal definition of the term? But in Cambodia, this is how it is. A legal abandonment is all that is needed for a child to become an orphan and to be given the name Rath. The name Rath means belonging to the state."

———————

While Molly gathered the children for play, Jennifer knew what she had to do. She quietly slipped away into the garden, far from the noise and the excitement of all the screaming and laughing children. It was twelve hours later in the United States, nighttime. Jennifer hoped her son, Greg, now thirty-two, and his wife, Myra, would be awake. She was about to enrich their lives forever.

"Hello, Greg. Sorry to be calling so late. Don't worry, everything is fine here. How are you guys doing?"

"We're fine," answered Greg.

"Listen. Is Myra awake? Can you put us all on the phone together?"

"Sure. Just a minute," he said. Jennifer heard him shout to his wife, "Myra. Pick up the phone."

"Hello. This is Myra."

"Hello, Myra. This is Jennifer."

"Hi. How are you?"

"Fine...I'm calling with some exciting news."

"OK. What's up?" said Greg.

"Well, a beautiful baby girl, an infant, was brought to the orphanage last night. I know that in the past we talked about your possibly adopting, and I was wondering if you feel ready to be parents. What do you think?"

Myra and Greg reacted as you might expect a young couple to. "Oh my goodness. Yes! What a pleasant surprise. When can we see her? What is her name? How do we do it, the adoption thing? We're ready! We are *so* ready. Thank you so much, Jennifer."

"Wonderful. I was hoping you'd say yes. OK. So I will e-mail you all the information, a picture of the baby, and a list of the things you'll need to do. Now that I know you want to do this, I will take care of the details here."

"Please send the e-mail as soon as you can. Greg and I will come to Cambodia whenever you say," said Myra.

"Very good," said Jennifer. "You have a good night."

"Thanks, Mom," said Greg.

"You're welcome," said Jennifer.

———•———

Jennifer walked from the garden to find Molly. She was playing the game Simon Says with the children. The nannies were playing, too.

"Molly, I need to speak with you. Can you meet me in the garden when you are at a stopping point?" Jennifer said.

"Sure. I'll turn the game over to the nannies."

———•———

Molly walked gingerly over to the garden. Jennifer was waiting for her.

"What's going on, Mom?" Molly said. "I saw you on your cell. Who were you talking to?"

"I was talking to Myra and Greg. I told them about Mona. I asked them if they would like to adopt her."

"Whoa! They said yes, I hope?"

"They did."

"Mom, are you sure you can promise this? After all, she just came into the orphanage last night. What about the ninety days? What if she is chosen by someone else? What if…"

"Molly. Trust me, Mona will become the daughter of Myra and Greg. And she will become my granddaughter."

———•———

Jennifer met with the nannies. "I have found a home for baby Mona," she told them. And they gave Mona over to Jennifer.

Jennifer and Molly left the orphanage with the baby and headed home to Jennifer's apartment in Phnom Penh.

"Mom. Are we permitted to just take the baby?" Molly asked.

"It's never easy, but it's what I do. All the necessary legalities will be completed at home. Mona will be safer with us than in the orphanage. I know how this seems, but it is the way it is done in Cambodia."

———

The Memo from Cambodia, August 2001

Myra and Greg woke up energized the next morning. Awaiting them in their e-mail was an advisory memo from Jennifer. It was informative—and surprisingly emotional.

Dear Greg and Myra,

So thrilled that you will be adopting Mona. Here is a photograph. I know it's not great, but I will FedEx you better pictures this afternoon.

I am sending this wonderful prayer, which comes from the words of Buddha. It's a prayer from you to Mona.

She is obviously too young to understand it now, but I know you two will cherish it forever.

"Dear Rath Mona. We promise to raise you in a home filled with love, so that you will be aware of your own Buddha nature—your basic purity that is your potential to become a fully enlightened human being. The seeds of love, compassion, generosity, ethical discipline, patience, wisdom, and other wonderful qualities already exist in your mind. We wish self-confidence for you that is based not on transient, superficial factors, but on a deep awareness of your own inner goodness. May you develop a kind and loving heart."

(I have sent this prayer to many adoptive families. I love it so much.)

OK. Back to business.

Please reserve approximately two weeks in December for travel to Cambodia. The time will be used for getting Mona a Cambodian passport, meeting with the US consulate, and taking care of general matters relating to adoption. Once you've picked your travel dates, I will schedule all the meetings you will need to attend. The plan is for you to return to the United States with Mona.

Book flights to Cambodia. You will fly to Thailand first. I will put you in touch with an American who specializes in travel to Southeast Asia.

Be certain you both have your valid American passports.

Bring cash for purchase of travel visas in both Thailand and Cambodia. The visas are to be obtained once you get to each country. Several hundred dollars will suffice.

I will call a social worker from Lutheran Family Service. She will contact you in the next few days. Lutheran requires an in-person interview, a home inspection, and a follow-up once the child has arrived.

Feel free to e-mail me any questions, and please keep me informed of your plans. Oh, I failed to mention that Mona is now living and being cared for in my apartment instead of the orphanage.

Love, Mom

"I wonder why Mona was taken from the orphanage?" said Greg.

"I'm sure Jennifer had a good reason. Maybe they needed her crib for another baby. Or maybe it's just standard procedure after an infant has been chosen for adoption," said Myra.

———◆———

The summer passed quickly. As Jennifer promised, the travel agent called to schedule flights to Thailand and Cambodia. Greg and Myra were to leave JFK Airport the evening of Monday, December 3, 2001. Approximately two days later, they would be in Cambodia. If everything went according to plan, they would be returning to America with Mona the week of December seventeenth.

Patricia, the social worker from Lutheran Family Service, visited Greg and Myra at their home.

The tenth of August had to have been the hottest day of the year. And of course, the central air conditioner was broken. The evaluation was surprisingly thorough. Patricia knew Jennifer, but that didn't seem to matter to her. Her demeanor was very businesslike. She inspected the entire house, including the nursery, the kitchen, the basement, and even the crawl space in the attic. She examined the aquarium in the living room. Her checklist was extensive, and she hit every line.

After the inspection, Greg, Myra, and Patricia sat around the kitchen table. Myra served tea with honey and scones. The scent of cinnamon sticks boiling on the stove filled the house. Greg shared the prayer to Mona with Patricia. She found it very moving.

Patricia took notes about Greg and Myra's income, expenses, mortgage, family members, friends, bank accounts—you name it, she asked about it.

Finally, Patricia was done. "You have a lovely home," she said. "It is clean and orderly. The nursery is adorable—I love the pink and green—and the sunlight coming in your windows tells me this is a happy home. But…"

"But?" said Myra. She and Greg held their collective breaths.

Patricia smiled. "I think you better get that air conditioner fixed. Come on, now. You can relax. I'm just teasing. You will make outstanding parents. Congratulations. You passed. And thanks for the tea and scones."

———•———

September 11, 2001. It was like a bad dream, only worse, because when we all woke up, we knew it was real. Terrorists had crashed airplanes into the World Trade Center, killing thousands of people. America would never be the same again.

First responders became a new and important classification of civil servants. Police, fire fighters, and emergency medical technicians.

The American government promptly went into action. Congress formed the Department of Homeland Security at the request of President Bush. Terrorism wouldn't be permitted to go on. Security measures were introduced on a worldwide basis. The US State Department reacted quickly. Visas were canceled for international travel nearly everywhere. Airport security slowed travel to a snail's pace.

Greg and Myra could only pray that their plans would be fulfilled. Would the September 11 tragedy and its aftermath settle down in time for them to adopt Mona in December? In Cambodia?

———◆———

Yes.

Greg and Myra traveled to Cambodia as scheduled. Jennifer met them at the airport with Mona. The new family got to bond for nearly two weeks. They became inseparable.

US Consulate officials met with them, reviewed their paper work, approved their adoption, and wished them good luck and Godspeed, all in less than fifteen minutes.

They returned home on December 18, 2001.

Shortly thereafter, because of the security measures implemented following the September 11 attacks, Cambodian adoptions were halted. Mona was one of the last orphans permitted to be adopted by US citizens.

I had to wait over five years for my second Cambodian granddaughter. But that is the story for my second book.

———•—

"Sayde Mona," said Greg and Myra. "Meet Pippop and Grandi."

I looked into the dark-brown eyes of my eight-month-old Cambodian granddaughter.

When she smiles, I melt.

To be continued…

Time Line: Modern Cambodian History
(Source: The Southeast Asia Resource Action Center)

1959   Vietnam War begins.

1965   United States sends combat troops into South Vietnam.

1968   North Vietnamese army retreats into Laos and Cambodia.

1969   United States launches secret bombing raids over Cambodia.

1970   Cambodia's pro-American General Lon Nol deposes Prince Sihanouk of Cambodia Prince Sihanouk aligns with the Communist Khmer Rouge.
        US and South Vietnamese forces invade Cambodia.

1971   United States continues its air strikes in Laos and Cambodia.

1972   Khmer Rouge army grows to 50,000 soldiers, many of whom joined to retaliate for the US bombings.

1973   Vietnamese and Americans sign the Paris Peace Accords. The Vietnamese begin to withdraw their troops from Cambodia. The last remaining American troops withdraw from Vietnam.

The United States stops its bombing campaign in Cambodia. Nearly 540,000 tons of bombs were dropped.

1975   Fall of South Vietnam; reunification of North and South. The Khmer Rouge comes to power in Cambodia. Approximately 34,000 Cambodians flee toward Thailand to escape the government-sponsored genocide, which results in the murder of nearly one quarter of the population.

1978   Vietnamese military forces invade Cambodia in response to border attacks, depose the Khmer Rouge, and install a Vietnamese-backed government. Hundreds of thousands of Cambodians escape into Thailand.
Cambodian refugees begin to arrive in the United States.

1979   Refugee camps open in Thailand to house some 160,000 Cambodian refugees.

1988   Vietnam begins gradual troop withdrawal from Cambodia.

1991   A formal ceasefire is adopted. The United Nations begins repatriating over 350,000 Cambodian refugees from the camps in Thailand.

1994   US embargo lifted against Vietnam.

Author's Biography

———

HERBERT J SHIROFF IS A retired 72 year old grandfather of five. He and his lovely wife Andi divide their time between Pennsylvania in the spring and summer and Florida in the fall and winter.

A graduate of Temple University, Shiroff is a member of the Temple University Business School Hall of Fame. He founded and served as CEO of the Mantis Manufacturing Company, producer of the internationally renowned Mantis Tiller/Cultivator. Many of the Asian refugees mentioned in RATH eventually found employment within the company.

Shiroff is a member of the Einstein Society, the research arm of the Einstein Healthcare Network.

He also is a member of Marjory's Friday Writers, a creative writing group based in Pompano Beach Florida.

CPSIA information can be obtained at www.ICGtesting.com
Printed in the USA
BVOW02s2201310816

460798BV00014B/158/P

9 781507 842348